OUR LOVE
COULD
LIGHT THE
WORLD

OUR LOVE COULD LIGHT THE WORLD

STORIES BY ANNE LEIGH PARRISH

SHE WRITES PRESS

Published 2013
Printed in the United States of America
ISBN: 978-1-938314-44-5
Library of Congress Control Number: 2013932194

For information, address:
She Writes Press
1563 Solano Ave #546
Berkeley, CA 94707

To John, Bob, and Lauren

CONTENTS

ACKNOWLEDGMENTS

The title story, "Our Love Could Light The World," appeared in the March 2011 issue of *Bluestem* and again as the final story in my debut collection, *All The Roads That Lead From Home* (Press 53, August 2011)

OUR LOVE COULD
LIGHT THE WORLD

The old lady had died some time that spring. No one knew exactly when because she'd been shut up in a nursing home forever, and then one day the son came around with a mover and that was that. The whole place was cleaned out. Minor repairs were done to the outside. As to the inside, it was hard to say for sure. People up and down the street who'd been there long enough to remember the old lady remembered a cramped, ugly kitchen, with Formica counter tops and a vinyl dinette set. While she was gone no one had lived there. The son came by every now and then and made sure things were okay, and people wondered why he didn't just take charge and sell the place. It wasn't as if she'd ever come back, the old lady. Once you went into a nursing home that's where you stayed. Until the funeral parlor, and that little plot of ground you hoped someone had been good enough to buy for you in advance.

Then the Dugans moved in. Although the street wasn't particularly close-knit—no block parties or pleasant potlucks—the neighbors welcomed them. Their efforts were ignored. The Dugans had moved seven times in the last ten years, and the idea of putting down roots was just plain silly. Soon the neighbors made comments. Not only were the Dugans unfriendly, they were noisy and didn't collect the shit their dog left wherever it wanted, usually in someone else's yard.

Mrs. Dugan left every morning at exactly seven-thirty. She got into her car, a rusty green Subaru, wearing a suit. Her hair was up in a bun. She even carried a briefcase. No one knew what she did. One man said she worked in a bank. The woman across from him said she sold insurance.

Mr. Dugan didn't work because he'd hurt his back years before on a construction site. The disks he'd ruptured eventually went back in place, but not before causing permanent scarring and calcium deposits, which caused pain that ranged from annoying to agonizing. He was never without pain, in fact, which kept him close to his beloved whiskey.

Five children made up the family. The eldest was Angie, a fat, teenage girl with a nose ring and short, spiky green hair. She ruled her siblings with a steady stream of insults. Her favorites were "dumbass," "dumbshit," and "horsedick."

The next in line was Timothy. The slight droop of his left eyelid was a painless affliction. He wasn't aware of it until people stared hard, then looked away in embarrassment. A baby-sitter once told him it was a gift from God, proof that Timothy was special. The baby-sitter was an old woman whose saggy chin sported a forest of short, white hairs.

Twin girls, Marta and Maggie, came just after Timothy. Mr. Dugan had objected to the German name, Marta. He thought the German people were fat, pretentious slobs. Far too young to ever have been directly involved in the Second World War, his sentiment stemmed from a boss he once had, Otto Klempt, who told Mr. Dugan he was the laziest worker he'd ever had in his storeroom. Oddly enough, Marta was rather like Mr. Klempt in temperament, harsh and scornful. Maggie was quiet on the surface, yet full of deep longings and desires she was afraid to share. One day, she was sure, she'd be on the stage, and very, very rich. Her husband would do everything for her—in her later years she'd see that she developed this idea from watching her mother bully her father—and she'd take every gesture with the same mysterious smile she gave her other fans.

The youngest was Foster. The name was based on a statement Mrs. Dugan made, that if she had any more children they'd end up in foster care. Foster had been born with a twisted leg that gave him a definite hitch in his stride, but otherwise did little to slow him down. He was a pleasant child, despite the generally sullen atmosphere of his household.

All in all, the five children didn't particularly care for one another, and they didn't dislike each other, either. One thing they knew was that they stood as a pack against the rest of the world, a term that had special significance after one of their neighbors came home to find them all roller skating in his driveway, where they'd apparently knocked over his trash cans in the process, and called them a pack of wild dogs.

He was punished for that. Paper bags full of dog shit, carefully collected over the week from their mutt, Thaddeus, were set afire seconds before a frantic knock on the door, made by Maggie, their fastest. Answering the call, the neighbor found the growing blaze and reacted as anyone would, by stamping it out. *HAHAHAHAHA,* the children thought to themselves, individually, in the privacy of their own thoughts, for that caper, like all their others, was born in committee, yet appreciated alone.

Angie felt the lack of community most. *We don't have enough family time* is what she concluded. She'd seen families spend time together. Across the street, the Morrises were always having cookouts, and batting balls, and playing badminton. The children—two, maybe three—laughed a lot. The mother never yelled, and the father had a strong, steady gait. She knew her own family could never be like that, yet she wished they could.

Mrs. Dugan came home from work tired. She was often crabby, too. She worked in the sales department for a small company that sold manufactured homes. Her job was to walk clients through their purchase options. The people she dealt with had all fallen on hard times, or were old and looking to downsize. None had the flush of optimism. Mrs. Dugan thought she herself had once been full of hope and ambition, which, over time, had been whittled away. She decided to give herself a kick in the pants, and when the chance came to represent the company at a regional conference, she put in her bid, and even took her boss out for lunch.

She was chosen. She walked on air. Mr. Dugan didn't like the idea of her spending three days down in Wilkes-Barre. He was glum, and snuck sips of whiskey from a flask he kept on a shelf in his closet.

"Three days, Potter. One, two, three," Mrs. Dugan said. She couldn't wait. She loved her family, and she hated them, too, and lately the balance had been tipping towards hate.

"And just what is it you plan to do at this conference?" Mr. Dugan looked like he was about to put his head through a brick wall, something Mrs. Dugan used to admire about him and now found exhausting.

"Attend presentations. Walk around the convention floor. See what other vendors are doing to improve sales."

"Sounds boring."

"Only a boring person would say that."

The stone face melted. His mouth turned down.

"I'm sorry, Potter. I didn't mean that. You're not boring."

"Yes I am, or you wouldn't have said it."

He took himself off to the small back room he called his den and lay down on the couch. He watched the dust dance in the light. Maybe three days wouldn't be so bad. Three days wasn't all that long. He could get a lot of good drinking done in three days. The thought cheered him.

Over dinner, Mrs. Dugan laid out the program.

"Angie, you're in charge. But don't you do all the work—share it equally. Start getting ready for school. There's only another week left. When you're not doing that, I want you each to clean your rooms. When you're done with that, take turns weeding the garden." The neighbors complained most about the garden. "And make sure Thaddeus gets his walks regular. I don't want to come home to a house full of dog poop."

Around the table the faces were still. The children had never been away from their mother before. Plans of mischief were being born, right there, as forks were lifted to mouths, and pieces of inedible pot roast were slipped unseen to Thaddeus below the table. Angie knew where her mother kept some extra money. That would come in handy when she took off for the mall. The twins planned to stay up all night watching TV. Timothy and Foster would live on ice cream and candy. They'd been handed a vacation, and they intended to make the most of it.

Mrs. Dugan packed her bag in a state of excitement and fear. She didn't have very nice clothes, although they were respectable. Which of her four blouses would go best with the brown suit? Or with the second hand lavender one she just bought? Where she'd never given much thought before to her appearance at work, she was now over-come with self-criticism and doubt. She had to look the part. She was an executive on the move. Secretly she yearned for a promotion, more money, and to get the family out of rental homes and into a place of their own. That thought made her sit down suddenly on her bed. The promotion might come, as might the money and home ownership, but the people who lived there would be the same—lazy, unkempt, and bad-tempered.

"Change your mind?" Mr. Dugan asked when he found her there some time later, still sitting. Some strands of black hair had escaped her bun and floated around her small, pretty face.

"No. Just taking a break." And with that she was up, finished packing, put her bag by the front door so she wouldn't forget it in the morning, and then shouted for her children to get ready for bed.

The sunlight that first day—Tuesday—said it would be hot. The house was not air-conditioned. If they were lucky, the children could get their father to drive them out to the lake and swim. They all liked going to the lake, except Angie. Bathing suits were devil spawn as far as she was concerned. One look at her father passed out in the den put an end to that particular plan. Angie said they should give Thaddeus a bath. The others agreed. A small, dirty plastic wading pool was put to use. Thaddeus didn't think any of it was a good idea and bolted from the tub the moment soap was applied and his fur scrubbed. He escaped the yard in no time, an easy feat since there was no fence, and bounded across the street where Mrs. Hooper was trimming her rose bush. Thaddeus stopped right in front of her and shook, sending water and suds everywhere. Mrs. Hooper shrieked and called the dog an ugly name, called the children watching from their porch an even uglier name, and then threatened to call the police when Angie turned around, bent over, and dropped her pants. No one came to fetch Thaddeus. Everyone knew from experience that he'd return eventually, which he did, the moment a can of dog food was opened in the kitchen.

After Thaddeus enjoyed his lunch and dropped soapy water on the floor, boredom returned. Foster applied a Band-Aid to each of his eyes—top to bottom—and groped his way through the living room where Timothy was on the floor coloring.

"What the fuck's wrong with you?" Angie asked. She was sitting in their mother's stained easy chair, flipping through an old magazine.

"Want to know what it's like being blind." Foster tripped over someone's jacket, collected himself, and continued, arms outstretched.

Maggie passed him in her ballet shoes. She was practicing standing on her toes. It hurt a lot. She thought of gliding over a dusty wood-planked stage to the silent, tense awe of the audience.

"Watch out, dumbass!" Angie said when Maggie lurched across Timothy. "Jesus, what's wrong with everyone today?"

Pizza was ordered for dinner. Afterwards all dimes, nickels, and stray pennies were gathered from every pocket, drawer, and stray sock. Mr. Dugan grieved. "Where the hell's my wallet?" When he couldn't find it he sat at the kitchen table and stared into space. The children recognized this mood. Their mother was both the cause and cure. She'd called to say she'd gotten there safely. Timothy had answered the phone. There was noise in the background, a man's voice, the sound of tinny music. Mr. Dugan took the receiver and told everyone to leave him alone so he could have a civilized conversation, for once, which he did for about forty-five seconds before Mrs. Dugan hung up.

At noon the following day, Angie went to dress and had no clean underwear. Foster lacked a clean shirt, and Mr. Dugan's sock drawer was empty. Monday was laundry day, and Monday was the day Mrs. Dugan had packed her bag. She hadn't done the laundry. Her oversight was painful to Mr. Dugan, because it strengthened his suspicion that his wife was essentially dissatisfied with her life.He called the children into the kitchen and told them to start washing clothes. Maggie took charge and trotted down the basement stairs. She returned to report that there was no more laundry detergent. A debate ensued. Could dish soap be used? What about shampoo? Angie told everyone to shut up, ordered her father to find his damn wallet, give her some money, and wait until she returned from the store.

"Let me go, let me!" Foster was hopping up and down. The store was a ten-minute walk, yet Angie doubted Foster's ability to success-fully choose and pay for a bottle of detergent on his own. Foster was only eight. She told Timothy and the twins to go with him. Safety in numbers, she figured. With four of them, not much could go wrong.

She jotted down some other necessary items on a list. Milk, bread, eggs, frozen fish sticks, ice cream, chewing gum, and mayonnaise.

"I want a candy bar," Marta said.

"Me, too," Timothy said.

"You get this stuff first. If there's money left over, fine."

The children left. Angie put the dirty dishes in the sink. The sink was full so placing them was tricky. She passed by her father's den.

"Angie! Hey, Angie! There's a guy on TV eating goldfish! What do you think about that?" he called out.

"That's pretty neat, Dad."

In her room—which was hers alone after a bitter fight with Mrs. Dugan about who would sleep where—she applied black nail polish with great care. She loved painting her nails. She loved painting other people's nails. She once painted all the nails of her siblings—including the boys'—a fiery red. The effect was stunning. Mrs. Dugan called her an idiot and demanded that it be removed at once. Mrs. Dugan had lost her sense of humor, Angie realized. There was a time when her mother laughed, danced about in her bedroom slippers, and bestowed gentle affection on her family.

Next she checked her cell phone. It was a cheap phone, gotten at great personal cost of begging and wheedling. Mrs. Dugan had been unmoved by Angie's repeated statement that all the kids at school had cell phones. Finally a low-end, poorly made cell phone with chronically bad reception found its way into Angie's loving hands. She liked to send text messages on it. There was one boy she sent messages to. The boy, Dwayne, had been in her math class the year before and she thought he was fabulous. She hungered for Dwayne the way she hungered for mint chocolate-chip ice cream. The messages she sent were bland, non-committal things like *TV sucks today. What's up?* His replies were equally bland: *nothing,* and *baseball practice,* and *cleaning out garage.* Yet into each she read a special meaning, a deeper truth that when added up in time would prove that he felt for her what she felt for him. There was no message from Dwayne. He hadn't texted her for two whole days, and her nerves were about to snap.

She texted her sometime best friend, Luann. *no mssg. from D. means what?* Luann texted back, *phone's probably off. or battery ran down.* Luann's brutal logic was painful, not comforting at all. If Dwayne cared so little about staying in touch that he turned off his phone, or let the battery die, then what Angie feared—that this relationship was completely one-sided—was true.

She shoved the phone in her pocket and went downstairs. The house was quiet. Her father had switched to a game show, and the sound of clapping and cheers was like a party from another planet. *Planet Party,* she thought, and wanted to write that down. Every now and then she made notes of random thoughts thinking that they, like the messages from Dwayne, would one day contain a brilliant and tragic truth about the human condition that only she was sensitive enough to see and appreciate.

The children hadn't returned from the store. The clock said they'd been gone almost an hour. She was furious at the idea that she might have to go looking for them.

"Boneheads," she said, and ate a slice of cold pizza left over from the night before.

Twenty minutes later, Angie saw the four children walking slowly up the street. Foster was in the lead. Behind him, Timothy carried a single bag of groceries. The twins followed, with an old man in between them. Each girl held one of the old man's hands. The old man was shuffling along, bobbing his head. His white hair was bright in the sun. He wore a plaid bathrobe over blue pajamas, and bedroom slippers.

"Jesus Christ," Angie said. She checked on her father. He was asleep on the couch. The television showed a muscular young woman in workout garb jogging through a park. The woman was smiling. Angie felt what she always did when she saw a body like that—deep, gut-twisting envy. She was thirty pounds overweight, and the last time she'd been to the doctor she'd been warned of the dangers of developing diabetes, which more and more young fat people were.

The children came through the back door with the old man in tow.

"Who the fuck is this?" Angie asked.

"We found him," Timothy explained.

"Found him? Where?"

"At the store," Marta said.

"Outside the store. On a bench, in the shade," Maggie said.

"Can we keep him? I think we should keep him," Foster said.

They put the old man in a chair at the kitchen table. His blue eyes were watery and empty.

"Caroline," he said, when he saw Angie.

The old man smelled of camphor.

"Why the hell did you bring him here?" Angie asked.

"We told you. He was on a bench. No one came out to get him, so we figured he was lost."

"Sir, what's your name?" Angie asked and peered hard at the old man.

"Caroline," he said.

"Great. Did you check his wallet?"

"Doesn't have one," Timothy said. Timothy was the most resource-ful of them all.

"He gave me a lollipop. There are more, if you want one," Foster said.

Sure enough, the old man had three lollipops in the pocket of his bathrobe.

Maggie put the groceries away. Angie saw that they'd forgotten the laundry detergent and the mayonnaise. And the eggs. She sat down. The day had become difficult.

"Well, he obviously wandered away from somewhere, so someone must be looking for him," said Angie.

"They won't find him. We'll hide him, and then say he's our grand-father, or something," said Foster.

"Are you out of your fucking mind? Where's he going to sleep?" Angie asked.

"With us. He can have the top bunk, and we'll share the bottom one," Maggie said.

"He might fall out of the top bunk. Better put him down below," Marta said.

"Caroline," the old man said.

"Sir, who is Caroline?" Angie asked.

The old man smiled. His teeth were perfectly white and strong.

"Is Caroline your wife? Is Caroline looking for you? Can we call Caroline?" Angie asked.

The old man looked at her vacantly. She might as well have been speaking Greek. She had to do something, but she had no idea what. The old man whimpered. He sounded like a puppy looking for its mother's milk. Angie ordered the twins to open and heat a can of soup. They argued about whether split pea or tomato was best. They settled on tomato. Foster tied a dish towel around the old man's neck. They put the bowl of soup in front of him. The old man looked at it and whimpered.

"Help him, then. Jesus," Angie said.

Timothy lifted a spoonful of soup. The old man opened his mouth like a toddler would. He took the soup, swallowed, and opened his mouth again. He consumed the entire bowl.

"Maybe he ran away because he was hungry," Foster said.

"He didn't run away, stupid. He wandered off. Someone didn't lock the door," Angie said. Then she realized that a search might be underway, and bulletins issued about the old man being missing. She went into her father's den and turned to the news. A tanker truck had exploded on an overpass in Indiana. A hurricane was speeding towards the coast of North Carolina. The President gave a speech about the economy to a crowd of angry, sullen-looking people. Closer to home, the local teacher's union had rejected the latest contract proposal. No one was looking for the old man.

Mr. Dugan opened his eyes. "What's up? I thought I heard voices," he said.

"Nothing. Go back to sleep."

"I'm ready for some lunch."

"I'll bring it to you in here."

"That's okay. I need a little stretch."

"Dad, don't."

"What? Stretch?"

Angie explained about the old man. Mr. Dugan sat up and stared at the worn rug at his feet. He nodded. He cleared his throat.

"You did the right thing," he said.

They both went into the kitchen. The old man's head had drooped down towards his chest. He snored loudly. Mr. Dugan said that if there were any soup left, he'd appreciate a nice bowl with a slice of buttered bread. Thaddeus stood by the old man's side, sniffing his leg. The other children were all seated at the table, each in his usual chair. The chair they'd put the old man in was Mrs. Dugan's. Angie prepared her father's lunch. Her cell phone buzzed in her pocket. Luann had asked, *anything?* Angie quickly wrote back, *no!*

"I think we should vote," Foster said.

"On what?" Maggie asked.

"On whether or not we're going to keep him."

"We can't keep him. He's not ours," Mr. Dugan said. "I'll call the police after lunch. They'll handle it."

"No! Daddy, don't do that. Please!"

"Now listen. This is a person, not a pet. Even if he were a pet, we'd have to find out if he belonged to someone else. In the case of a person, you can be well assured that he does, in fact, belong to someone else."

Mr. Dugan was proud of his speech. He was very sorry his wife wasn't there to hear it. The old man went on snoring. The twins got up from the table.

"Oh, well," Marta said. "Too bad." They went into their room. The boys stayed behind. Mr. Dugan called the police. His voice was bright and polished. He seemed happy. Angie wasn't happy. She was gripped by a growing sense of alarm.

"Someone will be along in a while," Mr. Dugan said.

"Do they know who he is?" Angie asked.

"No. They said it happens all the time. The nursing home might not even know he's gone yet."

"Assholes."

"Exactly."

The old man lifted his head and stared around him. He blinked. Mr. Dugan helped him from his chair and guided him into the living room.

"Come on, Pops. You'll be more comfortable in here. There you go. Want your feet up? No? Okay. Just sit there, and stay out of trouble."

Angie sat down next to him. The old man fussed. He plucked at the belt of his bathrobe and moaned.

"What's wrong with him?" Angie asked. She was afraid he was sick, or about to die. That wouldn't be good, if he just up and died on them. Mr. Dugan left and returned quickly with a glass of amber liquid.

"Maybe he needs a little nip," Mr. Dugan said

"What if he's on medication?" Angie asked.

"Won't hurt him." Mr. Dugan brought the glass to the old man's lips. The old man tasted the liquid. His eyes squinted and a gurgle rose from his throat. Mr. Dugan gave a thumbs-up. The old man nodded. He gave the old man another swallow. Timothy and Foster wandered into the living room. They were bored now. The old man didn't interest them anymore. Timothy picked up his coloring from yesterday, and Foster considered putting another set of Band-Aids on his eyes, then decided to wrap Thaddeus's toes together with masking tape. He'd done that before, and Thaddeus didn't seem to mind at all.

The old man held Angie's hand. His skin was very smooth, as if it hadn't touched anything rough in years and years. How long had he been like that? What, if anything, did he remember of his past?

"Well, I'm going back to my den for a little while, so you just sit here with him," Mr. Dugan asked.

"What if he needs to go to the bathroom?" Angie asked.

"You better hope he doesn't."

The old man had settled down. He fell asleep once more. Angie's phone buzzed. It was Luann.

going to the mall. want to come?

The old man's grip was surprisingly tight, so Angie had to type with only one hand.

can't.

why?

grandpa's here.

oh. text me later.

k.

Timothy got tired of coloring and went up to his room. Foster doodled on the back of an unopened bill. Thaddeus padded by, slightly impaired by the tape. Gradually Angie relaxed. She wondered what Dwayne was doing. She could text him and say, *guess whose hand I'm holding right now?* Then she wouldn't explain, and look sly when she saw him at school. That might shake him up. Dwayne needed shaking

15

up. Dwayne was too laid-back. She wondered what the old man was like when he was younger. Maybe he was as dull as toast until Caroline came along. Then Caroline turned his head. Caroline made him change his mind about everything. He went on breathing in a deep, steady rhythm. He might live quite a few more years, Angie thought. If he was well cared for, that is. Looking after an old man like that wouldn't be so hard, except for the bathroom issue. It occurred to her that wiping someone's ass might not be the easiest thing in the world.

The old man stirred, opened his eyes, and focused them hard on Angie. He smiled. He leaned towards her and planted a dry kiss on her lips. In a thin, wobbly voice he said, "Our love could light the world."

Eventually the police arrived and escorted the old man out. Angie held his hand until the very last minute. He was a resident of the Clearview nursing home, only a half-mile away. An employee of the nursing home had come in a separate car and told Angie about the service she'd performed that day, and how heartwarming it was to see a young person be so caring and responsible. Mr. Dugan emerged from his den and stood with Angie and the other children on the front porch and waved good-bye. Angie went to sit on her bed and think. Her mother would be home the day after tomorrow, and school would start the week after that. Time seemed like a slow, lazy river they were all floating along. Only the river in the old man's heart had flowed backwards, returning him to Caroline, whoever she was. To love someone so much that you'd never forget her, even when you'd forgotten everything else. That was something. That was worth having. As she checked her phone again to see if Dwayne had texted her, already knowing that he hadn't, she decided that one day, no matter what, she would.

AND TO THE ONES
LEFT BEHIND

Patty Dugan hit town at four-thirty in the morning with less than a quarter tank of gas and fourteen dollars in her wallet. The drive from Montana had taken two days. She'd slept in a rest stop in Iowa the first night, and woke up stiff and sore. The second night, in western Pennsylvania, was spent in a filthy motel room with shouting neighbors. She endured her discomfort with courage and profanity. It was her duty, under the circumstances. She was on a rescue mission.

No, I didn't run her off, her brother, Potter, said when he called. *She ran herself off.* He meant his wife of seventeen years, Lavinia. Patty wasn't a bit surprised. Lavinia thought she was better than folks, especially Potter. She had notions of self-importance. She thought her shit didn't smell. Potter was better off without her, Patty was sure, but she couldn't tell him that. He was a hopeless sop. He wept into the phone. He needed Patty to come and help. When she asked for how long, he said until the gaps were filled in. Patty had filled in those gaps before. Even though she was three years younger, she was the one to explain things when they were growing up—the washing machine, the microwave oven, and arithmetic, a subject for which Patty showed a marked aptitude and occasionally even enjoyed.

Lavinia had fallen in love with her boss, and she'd moved in with him. That was all. She hadn't taken any of the children with her. As far as Potter knew, she hadn't even told them good-bye. Then she called to say she expected to see them on some sort of regular basis, schedule to be determined. Potter said she had some nerve. What kind of heartless bitch was she anyway?

Potter's house was as desperate as Patty imagined. Weeds growing in the gutters, sagging front stairs, overgrown lawn, and were those actually empty beer bottles under the wilted rhododendron? All of this made visible in the dark by a very bright street lamp, as if the downtown Dunston community association had declared *here live the losers!*

Potter had instructed her to enter through a window in the back of the house if she arrived after everyone had gone to bed. Climb through a window? Please. But she did, because she thought of the sleeping nieces and nephews, though there was one room upstairs with a light on, Angie's probably. Angie was an early riser who seemed to awaken, without cause, every morning at four a.m., a trait that would have made her a great asset on her grandfather's dairy farm. As children, both Patty and Potter had been dragged from sleep in the dark every day to help with his herd. She'd hated it. If she never milked another balky cow in her life, Patty thought, it would be too soon.

Patty made her way over the paint-chipped sill, and spit a quick "Mother fuck!" as the window dropped on her shoulder. The family dog woke up, jumped off the stuffed chair it had been on, and sniffed her hand. Patty retrieved her bag from the porch where she'd left it. Then she moved a stack of magazines off the couch, lay down under the blanket Potter must have left out for her, and fell asleep. The dog joined her.

Patty was the hurricane, and Potter the eye. He sat still in the middle of her swirl, doing nothing but staring, and drinking when she let him, which wasn't often. She scrubbed the bathroom. She washed five loads of laundry. She threw out a month's worth of old newspapers. She walked the children to the bus stop in the morning, even Angie, who at fourteen didn't need an escort. They asked her about Montana.

Were there cowboys out there? Had she ever been to a rodeo? Did she know how to lasso a steer? She soon realized that her life out west had become a thing of legend. Potter, apparently, had talked her up. He'd given her so much flair, in fact, that they were surprised that she was only five feet two inches tall and thin as a rail. If she disappointed them, they didn't let on.

When she had time, she sat and thought. First about being back upstate New York again. Then she reflected on what had caused her to run in the first place. She was like that, logical in her thinking, and she liked to follow a solid line that sometimes led back, and sometimes forward. She figured she was meant for what Dunston didn't have, which was everything. That it was a man that had sped her away all those years ago hardly mattered, for she barely remembered him. Some blond dude with muscles, tattoos, and a car. A lot like the man she had now, she had to admit. Murph. Thirty-eight years old, worth nothing but company and occasional sweetness. Murph said if she left him alone, he'd fill his time with wild pursuits, which Patty took to mean women. She didn't think the kind of woman who'd take up with Murph was the kind who'd stick around for long, especially because Patty had put the money left over from the settlement in the bank. He'd gotten twenty-two thousand dollars for being tasered by a Helena cop with an abnormally high level of aggression towards panhandlers. They bought a nice trailer for $18,500: a double-wide with a bay window, a brand new dinette set, a new refrigerator, and freshly painted window boxes. The rest was in her name only. He didn't know it was there. She hadn't meant to deceive him, but rather to act in his own best interest. Murph was like a child tempted by an open cookie jar. In this case, it was best to hide the jar on the top shelf where he'd never think to look.

Lavinia took the children for the weekend. Patty got them organized. She encountered a surprising degree of resistance, particularly from Foster. He said Mommy had done a bad thing by running away and he wasn't sure if he still liked her or not. Marta said their mother needed a good kick in the ass. Maggie agreed. Patty said they were not proper ladies, and her comment seemed to shame them, because their gaze went to the floor and didn't lift again until they were at the door, waiting for their mother. Angie was indifferent. She hoped her mother would feel guilty and spend money on her. She was also a little curious about this boss who'd lured her away. Her mother always seemed like she had her head screwed on straight, not the kind to get taken with some stupid notion. She mentioned this to her brother, Timothy. He said *you can never tell what goes on with people,* a statement that impressed Angie with its truth and simplicity.

Lavinia appeared in a silver-toned jumpsuit. Her children stared at her. They were used to seeing her in a jacket and skirt for work, or in sweatshirts and blue jeans otherwise. Her hair was cut short and frosted with copper highlights. Her nails were long and red. She stared coolly at Patty as she ushered the children into her car—a late model SUV, not the beat-up Subaru she usually drove, solid proof that her fortunes had indeed improved. For a moment Patty wanted that car and she wanted it badly. She wanted to have nice hair, too, not the frizzy mess that fell around her face. Whenever she complained about it, Murph said cutting it would break his heart.

With the children gone, Potter hit the bottle. Patty gave up trying to keep him sober, and joined him. Their reconnection was slow and careful. In twenty years Patty had visited only twice, and not since Angie was a toddler. It was understood that Lavinia was to blame for that. Patty once called Lavinia a "royal bitch" to her face—not long after they were married—and things went downhill from there. They'd talked on the phone a couple of times a year since then, which let Patty feel like she really knew the kids she'd never met, and was why Potter had turned to her in the first place.

He wanted to know how Helena compared to Dunston. She said folks out there were as stupid as they were here, but the sky was bigger, the sun brighter, and the winters harder.

"I didn't think there was a place on Earth that had worse winters than here," Potter said. There was only a little whiskey left, and they moved on to a bottle of wine Lavinia had hidden behind the flour, where Patty found it the morning she made the kids pancakes. It was good French wine, probably a gift from the boss she was now living with, which made Potter reluctant to drink it at first. His reluctance, however, was quickly overcome.

"We got snowed in once, before we moved to town," Patty said.

"No shit!"

"Let me tell you, you really get to know someone when you're stuck like that."

"I bet."

"All the good, all the bad, everything."

She and Murph had been living way out in the country, in an old house owned by friends of Murph's parents. The husband got sick, and the wife moved them down to southern California to be near their son. Murph's parents put in a good word with the friends before they, too, moved out of state, in their case to Florida where they were both killed in a car accident two weeks after arriving. As heartbroken as Murph was at the loss of his folks, the real problem was that they'd agreed to pay the rent. They also had left their money, what little there was, to Murph's sister in Texas. She and Murph hated each other for wrongs done in childhood, which Murph never specified.

Patty and Murph had no choice but to go on living in the house. The electric company cut them off for non-payment, then the phone company did the same thing, which was fine since the friends down in California began calling to see what arrangements would be made now that Murph's parents were in the ground. Murph thought that was harsh. Patty said people had dollar signs where their hearts should be.

They decided to sit out the winter, then leave when the spring thaw came. The furnace being off wasn't a problem because there was a cord of wood stacked under a tarp in the back yard. Patty had a credit card they used for food. She made the minimum payment on it each month, which kept them solvent. They used lanterns for light. It was just like old times, pioneer days, except they had a car they took to town to do laundry.

A big snowstorm was forecast for Thursday. Patty loaded up on food and liquor and built a fire in the fireplace. They rolled out sleeping bags. They cooked on a propane camp stove. Looking back, Patty realized they were damn lucky not to have blown themselves up.

The snow fell for four straight days, and on the morning of the fifth the front door was stuck shut. They were both nuts from having been trapped inside. That's when Patty thought she might really love him. A man that could keep his temper was a beautiful thing. Murph crawled out an upstairs window with a shovel and cleared a path. He got so hot working he was down to his tee shirt by the time he was done. The trouble was they couldn't get the car out, and the back road they lived on wouldn't get plowed for another week.

"Weren't you scared?" Potter asked. Her story had brought a soft, wistful light to his eyes, and the liquor had put pink in his cheeks.

"A little."

"I've always wondered what Murph is like."

"He's good with a snow shovel."

Potter laughed. Patty remembered how the twilight that first clear day was like a blue tint on the whole world. She wondered what Murph was doing right then. She called him.

A woman answered the phone. Patty hung up. She might have dialed the wrong number, but she doubted it.

"That fuck," she said. She explained the situation to Potter. That was the wrong thing to do, because it reminded him of his trouble with Lavinia. Soon the light and glow were gone from him. He stared sadly into his empty glass.

"To forget all the good times. That's a sin," Potter said.

Patty had to agree.

The woman, it turned out, was their neighbor Francine. Francine and her husband Clay ran the little trailer park where Patty and Murph lived. Sometimes they came by for cards and drinks. Last night was one of those times. When the phone rang, Murph was in the bathroom. He called Patty back after she hung up on Francine.

"I miss you darling, something fierce. When you think you're gonna head your pretty ass back home?" he asked.

Patty was relieved, but not above calling Francine herself. Clay answered. Patty said she was glad that he and Francine were watching after Murph in her absence. Clay said they'd dropped down when they could, and that Murph was doing fine. He asked why she'd hung up the night before, and Patty said the connection was bad. Clay said sometimes he had that problem himself. He was thinking of getting a cell phone. His son overseas had one. Could Patty imagine that? A phone call all the way from Iraq on a cell phone.

Murph asking the old couple down to keep him company was even worse than his having a pretty woman in the place. It meant he was really, really lonely.

The children returned from their weekend in mixed humor. Angie was thrilled that her mother had given her fifty dollars. She was more thrilled that Chip—the boyfriend—gave her a hundred because he didn't know Lavinia had given her anything at all. She liked profiting from their sense of guilt—misplaced guilt, at that. She missed her mother only a little. Her mother had been, for the most part, a huge pain in her ass. Timothy couldn't stand Chip and didn't hide his feelings. Chip failed immediately by coming down the stairs of his large lakefront home wearing plaid golf pants. His nails were clean and nicely trimmed, and Timothy thought that a man should have rough hands, like his father's, which were always dirty, even though he did very little with them. Marta and Maggie liked Chip because he let them eat a bag of cookies and watch cartoons on the flat-screen television set in his own private study. Foster thought Chip was an idiot because he couldn't name the current Speaker of the House of Representatives—a question one of the other children had put to him for some reason Foster couldn't remember. Though Foster was only eight, he read the newspaper every morning. Listening to their report, Patty concluded that the children's opinion of Chip had broken distinctly along gender lines—the girls accepted him, and the boys didn't.

After getting everyone off to school that Monday, Patty poked Potter awake and said the time had come to face facts. He joined her in the kitchen a few minutes later. He looked like hell. He'd gotten pretty drunk the night before, and Patty had sequestered him in his back room so the children could come and go and not have to listen to his ramblings, all of which were about their mother.

"She's not coming back," Patty said. She put a cup of coffee in front of Potter.

"You don't know that."

"It's not what I know or don't know that counts. It's what she knows, and if I had to guess, she made up her mind a long time ago."

Potter pushed his coffee away. He went to his little study to play with his electric train set. It was a beautiful thing, over forty years old, which occupied the entire south wall on a table he'd built himself. He was proud of it. Damn proud, in fact.

Patty watched him shuffle off in his bathrobe. For one terrible moment she thought about inviting him and the children to move to Montana, then realized what a disaster that would be. She pushed the idea from her mind and took the dog for a walk.

Patty had been in Dunston for almost two weeks, and Potter was still trying to row without a paddle. Lavinia sent a check for one month's expenses. Patty was both glad and leery. Clearly, Lavinia assumed she'd be around that long to make sure it was properly allocated. Patty wanted to go home. Dunston had worn thin, and so had Potter's grief.

She called Lavinia. She wanted to know her mind. She said they could meet at the coffee shop in the mall. Lavinia said she'd have to check her schedule. Patty said she could check all she liked, but she better get her fancy ass there on time.

Lavinia was late. She wore another jumpsuit, this time red. The look in her eye was as hard as Patty had expected.

Lavinia bought herself a cup of coffee. She didn't offer Patty one. She smoothed her hair. Her heavy gold bracelets clanked. The boyfriend must be really loaded, Patty thought.

"Thank you for what you've done for my kids," Lavinia said. Patty was surprised.

"Well, that's why I came."

"I thought you came for Potter."

"Them, Potter, what's the difference?"

"There's a big difference. "

"Why? You left them all."

"I left *him*."

When Patty and Potter were kids, their mother reached a point of despair she couldn't talk herself out of and, like Lavinia, she left, but not for someone else, just to escape for a while. She went to a friend's, and Patty and Potter visited her there. The friend was a woman their mother sometimes sold eggs to, a widow, with a boy their age. Her home was comfortable, warm, and clean. Their father had told them to beg their mother to come back, knowing his words alone would have little weight. Patty found she couldn't. She wanted to stay there, with her mother and her friend. She asked her mother why she'd left them behind, and her mother said just what Lavinia had, *I didn't leave you guys, I left your fool dad.* Patty didn't see it that way then, or now.

"It hasn't been easy for them," Patty said. "They're at sea. They don't know what to expect. They need consistency."

"You know a lot about kids for someone who doesn't have any."

"I didn't come here to fight. So pull in your horns, listen to what I'm saying, and think about it."

Lavinia lit a cigarette. The coffee shop was non-smoking. She glared at the server who approached to remind her of that. The server retreated.

"I'm going to ask for custody. Chip says it's fine. His own kids are grown and gone," Lavinia said.

"What about Potter?"

"What about him?"

"You want to take his family away."

"They're better off with me and Chip."

"Have you asked them how they feel?"

Lavinia's expression said she hadn't considered that they wouldn't want to come with her and wasn't interested in hearing any objections.

"Look, I know how loyal you are to your brother, but maybe you should consider that this whole thing is his fault," Lavinia said.

"Sounds to me like you're letting yourself off the hook."

At that Lavinia leaned back in her chair and looked at her with a quiet, level gaze. Patty was taking an awful lot for granted, she said. Did she know that Potter hadn't brought in a paycheck for five years? Patty said he couldn't work, he'd been injured on the job. And he'd gotten disability, hadn't he? Lavinia said the disability ran out after a year. There'd been a chance for the payments to become permanent, but he'd had to file some paperwork with the state and never got around to it. That put her on the spot. She'd wanted to stay home and raise her kids. Potter had promised her that. That had been their arrangement. She had no choice but to get a job and leave the kids in Potter's care. He was hopeless around the house. She came home every day to an absolute mess. She showed him how to clean. The most he ever did was pull on her yellow rubber gloves and attack the downstairs toilet with an old shoe brush. She was always the one to mop and vacuum, and after a full day's work, too. And as for cooking a decent, meal, well forget that. How many times did he give the kids peanut butter and jelly sandwiches for dinner? Or hotdogs? Kids needed a balanced diet, for God's sake, so she had to take charge of that, too. Sunday was cooking day. She made big pots of spaghetti and sauce, macaroni and cheese, tuna noodle casserole, even a nice beef stew once in a while, and froze everything. She labeled what to eat on which day, and as Angie got older, she knew how to take stuff out, defrost it, and warm it up. Potter didn't even do the serving. Finally, one day, she realized she might as well be a single parent, for all the help she got. And as to the reason some people stay married, well, that was over between them long ago. And no, she hadn't been the one to lose interest. *He* did. Now what did Patty think of that?

Patty didn't know. Nothing Lavinia had said surprised her. Potter was just as Lavinia described. When Lavinia married him, people hoped she'd whip him into shape, and she'd clearly tried. He was forty-two years old, and he'd be the way he was now the day he turned eighty, if he lived that long. The question was, what to do with him?

"I still think you should talk to the kids. Sound them out," Patty said. But she knew they'd jump at the chance to live at Chip's, even though they didn't all think he was wonderful. They'd come around in time, if Chip put in a little effort.

"Already have. They're up for it."

"I see."

Patty helped herself to one of Lavinia's cigarettes, though she'd quit smoking four years before. She looked at Lavinia's hands and thought about them cooking, cleaning, washing, changing diapers.

"Tell me something. You love this guy?" Patty asked.

Lavinia shrugged. "What passes for love. He makes me laugh. We have fun in bed. And he works hard. Really hard. Self-made man, actually."

"He . . . what? Owns the manufactured home company you work for?"

"That, and a few other things. A car dealership in Binghamton, for one, and an Italian restaurant in Corning."

"And you have no more feelings whatsoever for Potter?" Patty wasn't sure why she'd asked that question. Maybe she wanted Lavinia to feel bad about having so much good fortune all of a sudden. Or maybe she just held out some wild hope that Potter's life would go back to how it had been before.

"Oh, I'll always care for him. He's the father of my children. He's not a bad guy. I just can't live with him anymore, that's all."

Patty hoped Potter's kids were tough enough to handle all the changes coming their way. They were tough enough for anything, she realized. In that way, they were like her.

"I guess you'll be heading back west pretty soon," Lavinia said.

"Yeah."

"That's too bad."

She seemed to mean it. Her cell phone rang.

"It's my honey, probably wondering where I am," she said.

Patty stood up. Lavinia talked into her phone and Patty said she'd see her later. Lavinia waved vaguely, absorbed in her phone call.

The kids were lined up on the couch, watching television. None of them spoke or even looked her way. There was a smell of food cooking. Potter was stirring a big pot on the stove. He was clean, his cheeks smooth.

"Didn't know I could make chili, did ya?" he asked.

"No."

"How was it?"

"What?"

"Your shopping trip."

"Oh, fine. Didn't find anything."

She sat at the table. The plastic mats were wiped clean. So was the floor.

"Looks like you've been busy," Patty said. Potter took a beer out of the refrigerator, removed the cap, and set the bottle in front of her.

"Lavinia never thought I could do anything, but I can. I do just fine," he said.

"Yeah." Patty had some of her beer. Potter got down a glass from the cabinet over the stove. His hands shook. It must have taken every ounce of strength to put on this show.

"Speaking of Lavinia, I've made a decision," he said.

"Oh?"

"I'm telling her that if she forgets all this nonsense and comes home right away, I'll forgive her."

"I see."

"Yup. That's what I'm going to tell her."

"When?"

"Just as soon as I get off my feet a minute and have a little drink."

He brought the whiskey bottle from the counter. It was a better brand than he'd had before. He was feeling flush from the money Lavinia had sent.

"After all, I can't keep you here forever, now can I?" he asked, and poured himself a glass. "You need to get back to that lucky fella."

"Well, you do seem to have things in hand."

"Sure. And Angie can always help me. She's a good kid."

"Potter."

"What?"

She couldn't say anything. She could see in his eyes he knew that Lavinia was gone for good. Anything from her now would tip him sideways, and he'd be there soon enough.

She missed Murph all of a sudden, worse than she had since coming out there. She missed their life, as messy as it was. She missed the way the air smelled, the sharpness of the shadows on bare earth.

"Well, to going home then," she said, and lifted her bottle.

Potter touched her bottle with his glass, drank all the whiskey it contained, and went to the stir the pot. One of the children yelled, and then a number of voices were raised in strife as the dog tore into the kitchen. Lavinia hadn't said what would happen to the dog, and Patty thought that if nothing else, she'd take him with her.

JUST ANOTHER LOST SOUL

The house was a Greek-style horror, the kind people loved to build back in the twenties, with tall columns on the porch and a large urn on either side of the front door. Inside, the black- and-white floor tiles reminded Angie of a chessboard. Foster liked to hop on one foot in a diagonal line along the white squares only. He had a phobia about landing on, or even touching, any of the black. Foster had the kind of intelligence that spun itself in circles, Angie thought, the result of which was that he'd been nervous and scared since moving in with their mother and her boyfriend, Chip. It was a bitter adjustment for them all. Timothy missed the ramshackle rental house he'd lived in when his parents were still together; Marta had loved the upper bunk of the bed she'd shared with Maggie, who pined for the family dog, Thaddeus. Thaddeus was now in Montana with their aunt, Patty, and probably having a rotten time. Only Angie was in good spirits. Moving to Chip's was an adventure, and so far she loved every minute of it. Sure, she missed her dad. That went without saying. She called him up every day from her cell phone and gave him cheerful words. *Chip's got a small head,* she'd report, and *His cologne makes me want to hurl.*

When Chip was home, he hid out in his wood-paneled den, playing solitaire at a large desk whose marble surface felt cold, even on hot days. It was understood that he was not to be disturbed. He wasn't used to children anymore. Those from his first marriage were in their thirties and never visited. Before Angie's family moved in, the entire house had been his alone. Angie wondered what it was like having your choice of any room to sit in and fart, if you wanted. Or shake your fist at heaven and rant about fate. Or dance around naked, drinking wine from a crystal goblet. When she imagined Chip doing any of these things, she broke down giggling, usually at the dinner table, which made her mother cast evil glances that threatened harsh punishment, though none ever came.

Her mother had changed. Before the move her words were sharp— *You, stop your whining. Timothy! Carry out the bags. Marta-Maggie, why is your hair not brushed? You've had over an hour! Foster, come here! Why are you crying? Get yourself out to the car this minute.* Now she seemed to sag, there in her place at table, next to Chip, who slurped his soup and sucked his teeth, and ran his hand over his greasy, thin hair and said, "Well, well!"

Angie liked having room to roam. She liked not having to share a bathroom with her sisters and brothers. She liked having a big closet, a double bed, and the small television set she put on her dresser. She liked being out from under her mother's radar. She liked being left alone.

The one thing she didn't like was going to school and having kids ask her how she liked her new dad. Chip wasn't her new dad. He hadn't even talked about marrying her mother, though she assumed they'd get to that point eventually. Then they'd go on a honeymoon, maybe someplace tropical and warm, and bring all the kids along and make it a family vacation. Or better yet, leave them home with Angie in charge. That whole house, under her control! There was a moldy old house-keeper, Alma, who stomped around, but she wasn't live-in, and Angie was pretty sure she could make a good argument for giving Alma a little vacation and letting her run things. She framed a speech about needing responsibility and wanting to prove her good intentions, the sort of thing her mother would have laughed at a year ago, but now would probably take seriously. Living with Chip had made her mother gullible because her attention was always elsewhere.

One night at dinner, while the kids chattered away about school and who would be what for Halloween, their mother sat silently, staring at her plate and eating little. Chip kept looking at her, and even reached out to pat her hand from time to time. That hand just sat on the tablecloth like a lump of dough. Her bad mood touched them all. Soon Maggie's lower lip turned down. She was remembering how they'd put red satin devil horns on Thaddeus one year and taken him door-to-door. Marta was wondering how she could coax a fancy princess costume out of their mother and realized that these days, with her being so grouchy, she would just tell her to go away and leave her alone. Timothy was glum, too, but not because of Thaddeus. There was a girl at school, the nicest-looking girl in the whole ninth grade, in his opinion, who had officially informed him, through one of her many messenger girlfriends, that any attempt to talk to her would be met with a slap on the face. Foster was worried about his mother and why she wouldn't talk, and what it might mean for the whole family if the reason were something bad. Angie was watching Foster, hoping he wouldn't cry. His feet were jiggling under the table, and the water in his glass was sloshing because of it.

Then their mother looked right at Chip. Chip nodded. She straightened up and took a deep breath.

"Kids, there's something I want to tell you. Some good news I'd like to share," she said.

"*We'd* like to share," Chip said.

"I'm happy to say we're expecting a blessed event."

Mouths stopped in mid-chew. Forks froze in the air. Under the suspicious gaze of her children, their mother's face reddened. Chip looked queasy, as if the floor were pitching like the deck of a ship.

"What does that mean, Mommy?" Foster asked. His voice was high and desperate.

"She's having a baby, stupid," Marta said.

Foster's little face pulled into a smile, and Angie was glad he was taking it so well, until she saw that he was miserable, and on the edge of hysteria. A moment later, he was out of his chair, tearing around the table, yelling, "You knocked her up! You knocked her up!" Maggie laughed. Then she, too, saw that he wasn't enjoying himself at all. Foster was in his socks because Alma required the removal of all shoes upon crossing the threshold. He skidded around one turn, then another, going faster and faster until he lost his balance, and fell—*splat!*—on that same black-and-white tile floor he hated so much.

Angie had him under the arms and on his feet in seconds.

"Calm down, idiot! It's just a baby," she said.

Foster wept. He struggled to free himself, but Angie held on tight.

"Take him to his room," their mother said.

"We'll do it! Let us!" Maggie said. Marta was already out of her chair.

The twins took Foster upstairs. Timothy asked to be excused. Chip said he could go, too. That left Angie, who was still standing. She stared at her mother, waiting for her to meet her eye, but she didn't. She was looking into her lap.

"That didn't go very well, did it?" her mother asked Chip.

"It's a shock, that's all."

"He'll feel better after a while."

"Sure he will. Kids are good at adapting."

It occurred to Angie that they didn't care that she was there, or rather, that they had forgotten she was. It seemed like a big thing to forget. She was torn. Part of her wanted to sit down and make them notice her, another part wanted to prove that she was indifferent. The indifferent part won, and she went upstairs. Chip and her mother sat talking a long time, then left the table without clearing it. They must have figured the housekeeper would deal with it in the morning.

Over the next few days, Foster came around. He didn't mind the idea of a new baby so much, especially when it was pointed out that he'd no longer be the youngest. The idea of having someone to boss had definite appeal. Nothing was said of his outburst at the table. Chip took refuge in his study. Their mother went to work, even though she didn't need the money anymore. Angie asked her why she hadn't quit, and her answer was, *I want to have a little something of my own.* From that, Angie saw that her mother valued her independence, and that she didn't expect Chip to take care of her. But that's precisely what Chip wanted to do. He was essentially retired. His business concerns—the manufactured home franchise where her mother was a sales representative, the restaurant, and the car dealership—more or less ran themselves. Or rather, he had capable people at the head of each. Angie's mother seemed to have come along at a point in his life when he was shifting gears. He wanted a companion, someone to go to the country club with and play a few rounds of golf. Angie's mother had just turned forty-one, and Chip was past sixty. Based on the math alone, Angie didn't see how Chip ever thought her mother was ready to slow down.

With the news of her pregnancy, Chip did the logical thing and proposed marriage. Angie's mother refused. She wasn't ready. A baby was one thing. A second husband was another. Chip was floored. Didn't she want to get married? Wasn't that the point of all of this? Angie's mother chose her words carefully. She talked about change, and how fast it came along, and how much time it took a person to get used to each speed bump in the road. *One thing at a time* was her message. He seemed to understand, though he was clearly disappointed. She didn't want to give the children something else to get used to. Children had to be handled carefully, she said. Chip thought the problem was that they hadn't been handled at all. They were the worst-behaved brood he'd ever seen, and one or more of them were always complaining about something. Timothy hated his math teacher and said it was her fault that he was failing the class. Marta and Maggie didn't like the lunches at school and wanted to bring sandwiches from home—made by someone else, of course. Foster didn't want to go to school in the first place and invented a new illness every other day. Angie wanted a lot of new clothes at the mall and didn't see why her mother couldn't give her a credit card. Her mother tried to explain how credit cards worked and how easy it was to get in over your head. Angie said in that case, she'd be happy to take cash. To this her mother sighed. Angie noticed then for the first time how dark the circles were below her eyes, and all the tiny lines around her mouth.

The children were divided. The boys thought their father should be told about the pregnancy, the girls thought not. Their argument was that it would only upset him. The boys felt he had a right to know. Either way, the problem was moot the minute Foster let the news slip. They were having ice cream in a place Potter used to take them from time to time. They crowded around a table meant for four. Foster sat on Potter's lap, and the twins shared a chair, though not quietly. Maggie accused Marta of having a fat ass, which she did, but hearing that made her pinch Maggie hard enough to cause a piercing wail. Angie told them all to shut the fuck up. They'd never bothered to curb their tongues in front of their father.

Potter put down his plastic spoon very carefully, as if it were made of fine crystal.

"Really. Well, what do you know about that?" His eyes were red-rimmed, not from sorrow, the children knew, but from too much to drink the night before. He'd shaved for the occasion, and cut himself in a number of places. His chin and right cheek had several small, circular Band-Aids that suggested an odd skin disease.

"She told us at dinner," Foster said.

The others remembered what had happened right afterwards and didn't say anything.

"It's good news," Potter said.

Foster stopped eating for a moment. "Maybe. Depends on if the baby is nice, or not."

"Babies are always nice."

"Was I a nice baby?"

"You were all nice babies."

The children considered this remark.

"Funny thing, though. She said she didn't want any more kids. Wanted to me to get a vasectomy," Potter said.

"What's that?" Foster asked.

"They cut the supply line," Maggie said, and put her fingers in the shape of a pair of scissors and snipped at the air.

"Gross!"

"That's what I said," Potter said.

He was looking glum again, and the children sensed that the visit was coming to an end. Once their father's mood soured, there was no improving it until he got a drink in him.

"Keep me posted on everything," Potter said to Angie as he dropped them off in front of Chip's.

"I will."

"And tell your mother—"

"What?"

"Never mind."

The children went inside, repaired to their separate rooms, where they each thought some more about what the new baby would be like.

The following week, Angie's mother was waiting for her when school was over. Her mother never picked her up. Some kids Angie knew got a ride in the morning, or in the afternoon, or even both, but not Angie. She had to wait out for the bus, no matter what, so seeing her mother there, in her shiny new car, was cause for concern.

"I have a doctor's appointment, and I thought if you came along, we could go shopping afterwards. You know, for clothes. For you," her mother said.

"Really?"

"Why not?"

Angie got in the car. Her mother smelled sugary, like overripe peaches. Chip bought her all sorts of perfumes and body lotions, which she felt obligated to try, at least once.

"Chip wanted to come with me, but I said, no, this was to be a girls' afternoon," her mother said. Angie realized the doctor must be an ob-gyn. Chip didn't seem like the kind of guy who'd go along for that kind of appointment, unless it was just to sit and puff out his chest and play the proud father-to-be. Angie had come to see that she didn't like Chip. She wasn't sure why. He put up with a lot. Maybe that was the reason. He seemed to let Angie's mother and everyone else walk all over him. Her own father was that way, too, but in his case, he couldn't help it. Her father was naturally weak. Angie couldn't see Chip as being naturally weak. No one who made the kind of money he had was weak at all.

The doctor's office was located in a one-story brick building near the university. The steady chatter Angie's mother had kept up since she got in the car stopped. Her silence continued inside, except for giving her name to the nurse. The waiting room had only one other woman in it. Angie and her mother sat with an empty chair between them. Angie looked at the magazines on offer, and settled on one about mothers and their newborns. She scanned an article about the benefits of breast-feeding. She put it down when she started thinking about what clothes to buy. She wanted leather boots, the kind fancy horseback riders wore.

"Lavinia Dugan?" the nurse called from an open doorway. Angie's mother just sat. When her name was called again, Angie nudged her.

"That's you," she said.

Angie's mother got up, and went along after the nurse.

While she waited alone, Angie thought about having a baby. For the most part, it didn't seem worth the effort. All that fussing and carrying on. The late hours. Her mother leaking tears from exhaustion and not even knowing until one of the kids asked her why she was crying. Angie remembered when the twins were born, though she was only five at the time. *A double dip,* her father called them, when they all came back from the hospital. A year later she was carrying Foster. She was so slight, you could tell right away that she was pregnant again.

Looks like she swallowed a melon, eh Ange? Don't you think? If Angie ever got pregnant, she wouldn't show for a long time, because she was fat. She didn't like being fat. She hated the teasing remarks, and the hunger every time she tried to cut down. But one day, if there were a baby, her body would make a good home. It would have plenty to eat up there inside her. She'd never get tired, because the extra weight wouldn't make a big difference. Afterwards she'd have lots of milk. Not like her mother, who put everyone on the bottle right away.

She ran her hands over her stomach and squeezed the soft, squishy flesh. Being fat just might have its advantages after all.

After almost an hour, her mother came back through the door. Angie followed her out of the office. They got in the car. Her mother drove towards Chip's.

"Aren't we going shopping?" Angie asked.

"No."

"Why not?"

Angie's mother stopped at a red light. The skin across her cheekbones had a yellow tint. She looked like sitting upright behind the wheel was a huge effort.

"I lost the baby," she said.

"Shit! Why?"

Her face was still. The light went green. She drove on.

"It just happened, that's all," she said.

Angie crossed her arms over her stomach. She pressed down until it hurt. Soon she couldn't stand how much it hurt, so she eased up.

"Are you going to be all right?" she asked.

Her mother slowed for a pair of children crossing the street, hand-in-hand. Her grip on the steering wheel tightened.

"Yes."

The children took a long time to cross. The bigger one was a girl in a pink jacket that was too warm for the day. The smaller was another girl in a sleeveless top. She dragged her jacket behind. The jacket flopped and bounced. It would be filthy in no time.

"Chip won't be happy," Angie's mother said.

"Of course not."

"But I have to tell him."

"Of course you do."

"He wanted me to have it."

"You couldn't help it."

Her mother's face tightened. So did her grip on the steering wheel. Her fingers looked dead, like wax. Then Angie realized her mother had had an abortion. That she *could* have helped it. That she'd chickened out.

Bye-bye baby. Nice knowing you.

Angie turned her head and stared out the window. A man raked leaves in his yard. His pile was red and orange. The color of fire, only stilled.

Why had her mother brought her along, and why the pretense of going shopping? Because she couldn't face what she was going to do, and needed back-up. She'd never relied on Angie for anything personal before, only for the chores she used to do when they all still lived with Angie's dad. Angie wanted to feel that her mother's counting on her for support was a good thing, that it meant she trusted her, and found she couldn't. All she felt was used.

At home they were met by the twins. Marta was holding a black-and-white kitten, and Maggie had a tabby one in her arms.

"What the hell is all this?" their mother asked.

"Tip and Top. Chip said we could."

"Really?"

They nodded. Angie didn't believe them. Chip said he didn't like animals in the house.

"We told him the baby needed someone to play with," Maggie said. Angie, standing behind her mother, drew her finger across her throat to signal that the topic should be dropped immediately. The twins took the kittens into the kitchen, where they'd set up two crates and newspapers.

"His car's not here. He must have gone somewhere," Angie's mother said. She didn't sound relieved. She didn't sound anything. Angie wondered what her body felt like, and if it had hurt. Her mother walked towards the circular stairs that led to the second floor. Her coat was still on, and her shoes echoed across the tile.

Angie's mother took Chip into his study that evening and closed the door. Angie thought it made sense that her mother would want to tell him on his own territory. Since they'd moved in, he'd acted as if none of the rest of the house belonged to him. He said *excuse me* if he came into the kitchen and they were there. Same for the living room and the basement TV room. Even if he passed them in the hall, he avoided eye contact. He seldom asked how they were doing, or what school had been like. When they had a friend over, which wasn't often, he made himself even more scarce.

Angie wondered if Chip would be mad—so mad that they'd have to move out. But her mother wouldn't say she had an abortion. She'd just say exactly what she told Angie, that she'd lost the baby. That was technically true, wasn't it?　And if he believed her, which he obviously would, then he'd never ask them to go. She wondered how her mother would talk him out of trying to have another baby. She also wondered why her mother hadn't been using birth control in the first place.

Because she was stupid. That was the only answer. Her mother, who knew everything and told everyone what to do, was just as stupid as the rest of the world.

Angie called a conference in her bedroom. The other four children, along with Tip and Top, assembled. Angie had a beautiful room, with a four-poster bed, a fireplace, and a large window with a view of the lake. Everyone sat on the thick carpet and took the news in stride. Foster wanted to know why the baby died.

"It just happens sometimes. There's a lot that goes into having a baby, and Mom had so many before, that maybe her insides are tired," Angie said.

"Sometime my insides feel tired," Maggie said.

"When you eat too much, you mean," Timothy said. That girl from school was on his mind again, and he wanted to go back to his own room and mope.

"Where does the baby go when it dies?" Foster asked.

"I don't know. It comes out in the doctor's office, and they put it in a tiny coffin," Angie said.

"And then they bury it?"

"That's right."

"When's the funeral? Can we go?"

"No. They had it already. This afternoon. Only the doctor and Mom went. I stayed in the car."

"Oh."

Timothy looked at Angie and rolled his eyes. She couldn't tell what the twins were thinking. They were busy with the kittens, who were swatting at each other's tails.

"I didn't really want another brother or sister, but it would have been okay," Foster said.

That was pretty much how they all felt, Angie thought. *Except me.* She was heart sore, and angry, two things she refused to reveal. She told them that the meeting was over and they could go.

Later her mother came in. She didn't knock first. She sat on the end of Angie's bed. She smelled of alcohol, and her hair wasn't as tidy as it usually was. She said Chip had taken it pretty well, though he was very sorry for her. She'd been through so much, he said, that it seemed unfair to suffer one more thing.

"Then do you know what he told me? Why he said he fell in love with me in the first place?" her mother asked. Angie thought she must have had a lot to drink to embark on this line of conversation.

"No."

"He said I struck him as a lost soul."

"Huh."

"He said I seemed like I was looking for something. An anchor."

"And he's the anchor."

"I know it's silly. But it's how men think sometimes, when they're lonely."

"Dad's lonely?"

"I know. I can't do anything about that now."

Angie wondered if her mother had ever tried. The idea made her tired, and she didn't want to think about it.

"What a day. What a goddamned day," her mother said.

The wind picked up, and a tree branch scraped the glass. They could be anywhere, Angie thought. Miles and miles away from Dunston, New York. Out someplace where the wind couldn't be stopped. Out where the wind really knew how to blow. But that was just pretend, because they were right here, in this pretty, fake room.

Her mother went on sitting, not looking at her. She pressed her fingers to her forehead. People said Angie looked like her mother, that she had her eyes and the same oval face, but she didn't think so. Her mother was slight and dark. Like Timothy. Some long lost relative, her mother always joked. Some rogue Italian. Her father was pure Scots-Irish, and Angie had inherited that red hair. The twins, too. Even Foster. Which made Timothy the outlier. Maybe Timothy was someone else's. Maybe they all were. Maybe no one belonged to anyone, and that was the big secret of the universe.

"Why did you change your mind?" Angie asked.

"About what?"

"The baby."

"What are you talking about?"

"You know."

Her mother looked at her hands. Her manicure was fresh. Her nails were a shiny lavender.

"I just couldn't do it," her mother said. "I thought I could. I really did. But I knew all of a sudden that I couldn't."

Angie thought her mother probably realized that she didn't love Chip enough to want to have his child. Even so, she should have kept it. There would have been more than enough love to go around from the rest of them.

Her mother went to her own room and Angie was left alone. The wind died down, and the night was perfectly still. This was the kind of night for lost souls to wander the earth. Looking for what, Angie couldn't say. Maybe for the ones that cast them off in the first place.

The baby was out there among them.

Don't look for her, Angie thought. *Look for me, instead. You have a home right here.* She pressed her hand just below her heart.

Then she felt foolish, and went to bed.

TROUBLE

Murph was pissed. He didn't like houseguests. Patty was firm, and laid it out one more time, in a clipped tone of voice that made Murph's mouth turn down. Her brother, Potter, was coming out with his eldest daughter, Angie, for a nice family visit. He'd only stay a couple of days, head back east, and leave Angie for at least another week, maybe two. How she was going to get home was unclear. The bus was an option, but Potter worried about her traveling alone. Patty said they'd drive off that bridge when they got to it. Murph had a bad feeling that this girl—this *teenage* girl—would crash there permanently. Her mother, Lavinia, just got married to the guy she'd been living with. The story was that he'd forced the point. Seems he didn't want just a live-in girlfriend, but a real, live wife, so he shoved the ring on her finger, as it were. A nice ring, too. Two carats at least. There was some conflict between the new stepfather and Angie. That's all Patty would say. Whatever it was had caused Angie to move back in with her dad, and that situation ran out of gas in just under three weeks. Now Potter needed a break. No job in over six years and living off his ex-wife. Nice gig if you can get it, thought Murph, who ignored the fact that his arrangement with Patty might raise an eyebrow or two because she worked and he didn't. It was Patty looking into the local high school that really got Murph going. She'd asked how late you could enroll a new student. When he put this in front of her, she put her hands on her hips.

"Jesus Fucking Christ, Murph. No one said anything about her staying permanently!" Patty had to admit that her nerves were on edge at the thought. She wasn't exactly the mothering kind, despite having, in essence, wiped Murph's ass for as long as they'd been together. But the kid was in trouble, and once again that sense of duty called.

Duty. Hard concept, that.

She bought bedding for the third bedroom, currently stuffed with Murph's shit. Once Murph thought himself a great blues musician, and his ancient L.P.'s, plus a ninth-hand Gibson with a hole in it, were collecting dust. She moved everything into the metal storage shed out back. Once the bed was made, and the new curtains hung, she knew she'd overdone it. Angie didn't seem like the kind to love roses and daisies on everything, but that's what K-Mart had had on sale, so that's what she had to look forward to. As for Potter, the couch was fine for him. The second bedroom was Patty's to use when she couldn't bear the sound of Murph's snoring any longer. And for those nights when she needed to stretch into the empty space around her without bumping into Murph's bulk. In other words, when she had to be alone.

In further preparation for their arrival, Patty ordered Murph to give the dog a bath. Thaddeus was a black, curly-haired mutt, who tended to stink no matter what. Patty had taken him back to Montana with her after she left Dunston the year before. She knew damn well Potter wouldn't do right by him, though in Thaddeus' case, doing right amounted to nothing more than canned food twice a day and being let out to pee and shit. Patty tried to train him to sit and stay, and come when she called, but he did nothing but stand and stare at her.

Murph felt a kinship to that dog. He thought his trouble—and the dog's, too—was a woman asking too much of them. Men had to be independent and left alone to go a little crazy from time to time. Craziness was not permitted in Patty's home. Only in her heart, which could change faster than the weather in Helena. One day her love tap ran hot and steamy, and the next it iced up and broke. Murph had no doubt at all that if Patty would love him the way he loved her, he'd have his feet a lot more on the ground. She nagged him because he was restless and unsettled, and he was that way because when he needed to know that she was the one thing in the whole world that would never change and would always be there, she shifted the ground beneath him just enough to throw him off balance.

Patty was going places. She'd been promoted to manager at the Dusty Boot, a two-bit bar and grill out on Highway 12. She'd fired about half the staff and replaced them with younger people, mostly Mexicans, who couldn't always produce a green card, which didn't bother Patty as much as Murph thought it should. It riled him to think of illegals getting work when he couldn't, which made Patty suggest that he come on down and try his hand at peeling potatoes or washing dishes. As if. Then she upgraded the menu with the help of a restaurant consultant, some dude from Las Vegas who stopped in on his way out to Seattle. They got to talking—Patty believed in taking the friendly approach with anyone who seemed like he had a bit of money—and he said he admired the look of the place with its old-style red leather booths and wagon wheels up on the wood-paneled walls, but found the offerings a bit limited. Which meant basically steak and potatoes, with a salad bar. Patty had been put out. She said that their desserts were some of the best around and gave him a free slice of key lime pie, which he agreed was first-rate. Even so, if she wanted to attract a different sort of clientele, say government folks, or some of the wealthier landowners who'd been a place or two, she had to think more upscale. A.k.a. more green salads with goat cheese and roasted red peppers, that sort of crap. So Patty went to the owner, Bald Bill, Murph called him. Bill was all for change—if it made him money. *It takes money to make money,* Patty said lamely after she'd figured the cost of all those fresh ingredients. Finally Bill came around. Murph was pretty sure Patty exchanged a few favors for his signing off on her expansion plans, but she denied that vehemently. So vehemently that Murph spent two nights in the bed of his pick-up truck. Long story short, Bald Bill wrote the checks, Patty made the deals, and people came in to eat a lot more than they did before.

What Murph really wanted to know was how Angie would fit in.

"We'll figure it out. That's what life is, figuring shit out," Patty said.

"Not my life."

Patty's hands went to her hips again.

"Okay, okay, don't get your knickers in a twist," he said. At that point he hauled the dog outside and washed him in an old plastic tub he used to keep his beer on ice.

The first problem Angie had was the weight she'd put on. She'd never been slim according to the pictures Potter faithfully sent every year from Dunston. Patty had a whole album full of Potter's five kids as they rose through the ranks of the Dunston school system. As a baby Angie was robust. By the time she was five, her shirts rode up over her round, white stomach. Her arms were softs and doughy. Even an adolescent growth spurt didn't trim her down. She'd been stable for a while, then whatever happened to upset her so much made her stuff herself double-time. Something had changed in her soul, too. She didn't want to meet your eye. She used to be sharp-tongued and bossy as hell. Now she sat quietly and barely spoke. Patty saw right off that she was going to have to get to the bottom of this, but with her brother around, that would be difficult.

The first night Angie turned in early, and Potter and Patty stayed up. Murph had bailed out to a local bar where they played bluegrass. Potter had showered and shaved. His red-blond hair, neatly parted and combed, was streaked with gray. He was still a handsome man, Patty thought. And he hadn't run to fat, either. At the moment they were on their third round. Potter was taking it easy, which meant he was sipping his whiskey and not belting it back the way he had the year before, when Patty visited Dunston.

"So," Patty said.

"So."

"She seems okay."

"Comes and goes."

"What happened back there, anyway?"

"Won't say. But, if you ask me, I think that s.o.b. made a pass at her."

"Are you kidding me? An old guy like that?"

"No age limit on perverts."

It was Timothy who brought it all to light. One evening around bedtime, he saw Chip coming out of Angie's room with an awful look on his face. Inside, Angie was in a bathrobe, naked underneath. Her face was awful, too, with some tears added in. Timothy asked what had happened. Angie said nothing, even when asked two more times. Angie was a big girl and could take care of herself, so Timothy let it drop.

In the end, it was her silence that made him speak. Angie never held her tongue about anything that upset her. The whole world knew what was on her mind and always had from the moment she could talk. For her to go mute like that meant that something major had rattled her cage. When Potter said this, Patty could see how much he loved her.

"Did you ask her flat out if the creep put a hand on her?" Patty asked. The summer night glowed silver from the nearly full moon.

"No."

"Then I will."

"Not sure that's a good idea."

"Why the hell not?"

"Well, I asked a therapist friend of mine about it, and he said sometime it's best to let a person find the words on his own."

"You have a therapist friend?"

Potter's face said he wasn't going to say anything more on that particular subject. As they sat, not talking for a few more moments, Potter looked around the kitchen they were in, and out into Patty's living room. His eyes were sad.

"You've done all right. This is a nice place," he said.

"I keep it that way. Murph's kind of a slob."

"He's a guy."

"True."

Potter sipped his drink and savored it.

"You two ever going to tie the knot?" he asked.

"Nah."

"How come?"

"Don't see the point. As it is, I got all the advantages of marriage with none of the headaches."

The moment Patty said this, she realized she'd gotten it backwards. Living with Murph gave her all the headaches, and none of the benefits of marriage. Potter seemed to see that too, from the way his eyes quickly met hers, then looked away as he went on relaxing into his drink.

By the following Tuesday, Potter was on his way back to Dunston, singing along to one country song after another in his rusty sedan. He thought his visit went quite well. Murph took him to a bar on his last night, and Potter couldn't remember how he got home. He greatest talent, other than loving his children, was an immunity to hangovers. He was confident that whatever harm Angie had suffered, Patty would put it right. That was Patty's talent, putting things right. He'd be in bad shape today if she hadn't helped him out last year, right after Lavinia took off. Something about Patty's no-nonsense approach to everything helped ease the bitterness he felt. Lavinia had been a pain in the ass to live with, and that was the truth. Without Patty, he might never have really seen that.

Potter wasn't three miles down the highway when Angie discovered a small can of black paint that Murph had used on the window trim the summer before, and applied it to the walls of her new room. Next came black curtains, a black bedspread, black sheets, and a round shaggy black rug with a rubber back, the kind you'd put in a bathroom. When Patty got home from the Dusty Boot and saw what Angie had done, she asked if she'd like her to tack an upside down cross above her bed.

"That's not funny," Angie said. She felt stupid, not for her color choice, but because she'd run through so much of the money Potter had given her.

"Neither is this. Before you go throwing paint up on someone else's wall, you need to ask if it's okay."

"Is it okay?"

"No."

"Why not?"

"Because it looks like shit."

Angie wished she had a candy bar. That's one thing she hadn't bought on her spree. She sat down on the bed. She refused to cry.

Patty was mad at herself. She didn't want to play the heavy. She wanted to be kind and understanding, and have a "just between us girls" sort of thing with Angie. That wasn't going to be possible, though. Patty knew people her own age who tried to be friends with their teenagers, when what they needed was to be their parents—which didn't necessarily mean being a jailer, either. Just—what? A voice of reason and common sense.

"I think a contrasting color would be nice, given how dark everything else is," Patty said. Angie was into dark. Patty had helped her unpack, and of the ten tee shirts she'd brought nine were black with some kind of graphic, like a skull, or a skunk, or a pair of bloodshot eyes. The other was gray and with a bloody hand on the back.

"Like what?" Angie asked.

"How about red?"

"Black and red are my school colors."

Patty didn't have to ask if that were good or bad.

"Orange, then," she said.

"Too much like Halloween."

"Green?"

Angie gave that some serious thought. Green and black reminded her of something dashing and strong, she didn't know exactly what. In the end they chose light blue because Patty said there was a rare kind of butterfly found only on the Montana prairie with that same color combination, a notion that appealed to Angie. Patty hoped to hell she'd never have to produce a picture of that butterfly, because it didn't exist. She was tired of offering up options, only to have them met with a sour expression that reminded her so much of Lavinia she poured herself a small shot of whiskey the minute she left Angie's room, though it was only two in the afternoon.

Murph offered to help his buddy Kevin move just so he could have a day out of the house. Kevin was bound for his grandmother's in Missoula for the fall, where she lived alone in a large place he'd agreed to renovate in exchange for free rent. Kevin didn't know anything about renovating houses, but figured it couldn't be all that hard, and if it were, he'd call on Murph, who was pretty good with tools when he wasn't drinking or fighting with Patty.

"What do you mean, creepy?" Kevin asked. They'd just wrestled a very heavy set of free weights into the U-Haul which Murph had to think Kevin had never used, given that he couldn't lift for shit, which was less than convenient at a time like that.

"She watches me. All the time, those round little eyes are on me," Murph said.

"She thinks you're hot."

"Eat shit."

Angie didn't look at Murph with lust. He knew what a woman's lust looked like. There was no glow in her cheeks, no soft light in her eyes, and her lips were pressed so hard together they made a straight line. He wouldn't be a bit surprised if one day she jumped up and clawed his face, and that's exactly how he put it to Patty. *You probably scare the crap out of her, the way you clomp around and swear all the time. And the way you fart at the table probably isn't boosting her confidence, either.* Okay, so he was crude. Who had a better right? It was his house, wasn't it? If she didn't like it, she could take her fat little ass on down the road, though he didn't say a thing about that to Patty. He wasn't looking to get slapped.

Kevin said they'd earned themselves a pitcher of beer, and Murph couldn't disagree. After a few glasses the answer was clear. He'd just avoid her. Given how small the trailer was, he wasn't sure how he was going to do that, but he'd find a way.

Patty thought it would be a good idea for Angie to learn something of the larger world, so she took her down to the restaurant and showed her the ropes. She had her observe the waitresses taking meal orders, the cooks preparing them, the bus boys, the cashier, and then she ran her through her own routine—payroll, inventory control, ordering from suppliers, and even had her come along for a meeting with their banker about extending the restaurant's line of credit.

"We want to renovate the interior. Something a little sleeker and more modern," Patty explained as they drove. "The trick is to keep making money while the work's going on. That means we'll have to offer lots of specials to keep folks coming in. I'm thinking a two-for-one deal on entrees every Friday, and half-priced drinks, too. What do you think?"

"Sounds fab," Angie said. She was so bored she could spit. Patty had made her put on a dress and closed-toe shoes. She'd also been required to remove the nose ring and lip stud she normally wore. Patty was wearing a polyester suit that was baggy in the ass. Angie thought if she were so bent on looking the part, she might find a better place to buy her clothes.

When they got to the bank, Angie sat in the lobby while Patty made her pitch to a guy who looked about twenty years old, at a desk tucked in a corner behind a column. Five minutes later Angie was out the door. Her shoes were impossible to walk in, so she removed them and threw them in a dumpster. Home was almost four miles away. She stood with her thumb out sweating in the heat, until some old guy in a cowboy hat picked her up.

"Where'd you lose your shoes, Little Lady?" he asked after she climbed in. Angie didn't answer. He talked about the weather, and how you could tell that the winter ahead was going to be a cold one from the way the cattle were behaving (he didn't specify what aspect of their behavior suggested this); about his married daughter in Minneapolis who was training to be a cop; about his late wife and her passion for putting up fruit. Angie realized that everyone in the state of Montana was insane, and that coming there was a mistake. Going back to Dunston was a bigger mistake, so she sat and thought about a third choice—finding a new place entirely, California maybe. That presented the usual problems—money and transportation. Patty had money in the bank, or at least she hinted she did. That was an angle Angie could work. She'd have to smooth over this afternoon first, though.

"Oh, Aunt Patty, I'm sorry I left like that, I wasn't feeling too good. I think I ate something bad at the restaurant," Angie said. She was lying on the couch with a rag on her forehead to emphasize her weakened state.

"How the hell did you get home?" Patty asked. Her face was red up to the roots of her wild, frizzy blonde hair.

"I caught a ride."

"I see. Well, from now on, you do NOT walk off like that. You do NOT hitchhike. You LEARN a sense of responsibility!"

Angie sat up, once again glum. She'd never liked getting yelled at.

"Jesus, I could hear you down the street," Murph said as he opened the front door. His tee shirt was dirty. So were his hands. He'd been helping another friend with some landscaping. The friend said he'd pay him, but Murph had refused. That was something Patty intended to take up with him at the earliest possible moment.

"Give us a minute, would you?" Patty said. She was still standing in front of Angie. Murph went down the hall to take a shower. Patty kicked off her high heels. The meeting with the banker hadn't gone too well. He wanted to see more statements—a profit and loss, to be exact. Patty was a seat-of-the-pants person who had no formal training in bookkeeping or accounting, something Bill had suggested she might look into. Either that, or hire someone, which would cost more money, and that seemed to defeat the purpose.

"I've tried hard with you. Now you have to try," she told Angie.

"Meaning what?"

"What I just said. Stay in touch. Open up. Speak your mind."

"This place sucks."

"This place is no better or worse than any other place. You can be just as happy here as you can be anywhere. It's up to you."

Patty sat down on the coffee table. She wanted to soften her tone.

"You wanted to come out here, right?" she asked.

"I just wanted to get away, that's all. This was my dad's idea."

"I see." Patty needed a drink badly and knew this wouldn't be the time to get up and pour herself one. Murph was singing in the shower. He was an absurdly happy person, sometimes. It drove her a little batty.

"You know, when I was a kid, back in Dunston, there was this guy who sometimes helped my dad out on the farm. Named Mr. Norberg. He was . . . friendly. A little too friendly, sometimes. He always patted my head, or put his arm around my shoulder, and I thought it was sort of weird," Patty said.

"Weird?"

"Well, yeah. A little too familiar. I mean, it's not like he was a relative, or anything like that."

Angie didn't seem the least bit interested in what Patty was trying to tell her.

"So, one day I told my dad. And Mr. Norberg didn't work for us anymore," Patty said.

"Just like that?"

"Pretty much."

Down the hall the shower turned off. Murph went into the bedroom and closed the door. Thaddeus padded in from the back porch and stuck his nose in Angie's hand. Angie ignored him.

"Don't you want to tell me what happened?" Patty asked.

"When?"

"You know when."

At that Angie got up and went into her black and blue room.

One week stretched into two, then three. Potter called to see how it was going. Lavinia didn't call at all. Angie texted her little brother, Timothy, the only one of the kids who had a cell phone, and he passed her messages down to the twins and Foster. They all missed her and wanted to know when she'd come home. Angie said she didn't know, and that they shouldn't be lonely without her. She also said to steer clear of Chip, which they all did anyway. Then late one night Timothy called. Angie was still awake, flipping through some stupid book on self-esteem that Patty had left on her bed.

"What's up?" she asked.

"Nothing. What's up with you?"

"Why are you calling?"

"You know, stuff." He asked when she was coming home.

"Dunno. Might start school out here," she said.

"With a bunch of cowboys and cowgirls."

"Not everyone is like that."

Angie had made one friend, a Mexican girl who worked at the Dusty Boot. Rosita was determined to become as American as possible and wanted Angie to teach her everything she needed to know. She dyed her hair blonde, wore pink lipstick and tank tops that made the busboys stare and whisper to each other. She chewed gum, until Patty put a stop to it. She got herself an iPod and hung out at the drive-through burger place, until some white boy made an ethnic slur, which sent her into a fury. Angie had to persuade her to drop the brick in her hand, found miraculously below one of the outdoor tables.

"They're back from their honeymoon," Timothy said.

"Big fucking deal."

"Mom was tan. Chip looked fatter."

Angie didn't know why he was telling her this.

"They took us out for dinner," he said.

"Joe's, no doubt. Did you love your cold, sticky spaghetti?"

"We went to Madeline's."

That was the fanciest restaurant in all of Tompkins County, and the priciest. Angie's heart sank at the thought of the drippy, chocolaty desserts that came on little white plates, set down with a graceful swoop upon a deep red tablecloth. Or so she'd heard. She'd never been there, herself.

"Chip made a toast. Tapped his knife on his glass and the whole thing. Mom told him to be careful, or he'd break it."

The laughter edging Timothy's voice made Angie's skin hurt. Something clawed on the roof overhead, an owl, she figured, from the way it showed up every night at about the same time. Murph said there were a variety of owls in Western Montana. Murph was trying to be nicer. Angie figured it had something to do with the number of nights Patty had spent by herself in the spare room. She told Timothy to take care, and say hi to the others. She hung up.

Patty noticed Murph's improved attitude, too. She told him that Angie was probably going to stay on for a while, just as he'd predicted, that she was sorry, but thought that the three of them could make a decent little family. Murph wondered if that was her way of saying she was thinking about having a kid of her own. It wasn't. Patty had given up on that notion long ago, not for anything that had to do with Murph (and the fact that he was shiftless), but because she knew, in her heart, that she wouldn't make a good parent. She learned that all over again when Angie first came. She was quick to anger and tended to bark out her opinions like orders. But Angie was on her way to becoming a young lady who, in time, would be more like a roommate than a child.

In the spirit of cooperation, Murph offered to take Angie with him to work one day. He was still planting shrubs at some rich guy's place.

"You don't have to do anything major, just drag the hose around, water those puppies once we get them in the ground," he said.

Angie thought it sounded boring. Patty packed them each a lunch of bologna sandwiches, potato chips, and a chocolate chip cookie. Murph would have preferred something decent from the restaurant, but Patty seldom brought home leftover food. She let the kitchen staff have first choice, and there was never anything to spare, or so she said.

Alone, Patty's mood was good. Things were working out. She was happy to see Murph making an effort, and Angie, too. She thought of putting in a call to Potter to say how she was doing and decided that later today, when Murph and Angie returned, Angie might want to do that herself.

It was almost six when Murph's truck pulled up. Angie came through the door, her face dirty, her hair snarled, and went straight into the bathroom without a word. Murph stood in the doorway until Patty asked him what the hell was wrong. He came in and joined her at the kitchen dinette set. His face and hands were dirty, too.

"Listen," he said.

"Well?"

"I don't know how to make you understand this, but there is something seriously wrong with that kid."

"Like what?"

"She put the moves on me."

"What?"

"On the way back here, she put her fucking hand on my knee and asked if she could suck my cock."

Patty put her glass of scotch onto the table. She stood up carefully, pushed her chair in, went to the cabinet where the glasses were kept, removed another shot glass, filled it with whiskey from the bottle next to the toaster, came back to the table, and just as carefully pulled out her chair and sat down. She put the glass in front of Murph.

"You don't believe me," he said.

"Yes, I do."

"You do?"

Patty glanced down the hall to see if Angie might be standing in the hallway, trying to overhear their conversation. She wasn't.

"Of course. It's the only thing that makes sense," she said.

"Of what?"

Patty told him what Potter had suggested, that Chip had tried to nibble from the wrong honey pot.

Murph tasted the whiskey she'd given him. The shower started up in the bathroom. He was afraid of what would happen when it stopped.

"Only I don't think it happened quite that way," Patty said.

"No?"

"He just got Lavinia and her brood on board. I'm sure she serves him well enough in the wet-dick department, so why would he risk that by taking a swipe at Angie?"

Murph didn't know. Angie scared the crap out of him. Any guy would be well advised to steer clear of her.

"On the other hand, Angie stood to gain by trapping Chip. Her mom would get so pissed he'd never get on her good side again," Patty said.

"Maybe. But why would she want her mom pissed off? And what's that got to do with wanting to blow me?"

"She'd say you made her do it, and that would flip me out and put a permanent wedge between us."

The next sip went down well and made a warm spot in his gut.

"Why would she want us to get crosswise?" he asked.

"Just for the sake of making trouble."

Murph drank his drink. He stank of sweat. Patty didn't mind. She felt like something the size of a bowling ball had been hollowed out of her stomach.

"So now what?" Murph asked.

"She's outta here." Patty wondered how she was going to make Potter understand why Angie was coming home all of a sudden. Hearing the truth wasn't something he was very good at. Maybe she'd just say having her hadn't worked out, or that she'd wanted to leave. That way Angie would be the one to explain what had happened. Only fair, under the circumstances.

When Murph wiped away her sudden tears, he left a smudge on her cheek. How sweet she was, he thought. Underneath everything, Patty had a strong, loving heart that for once had shifted in the right direction. He was glad it would be just the two of them again. He'd always thought that's just how it should be.

A SIMPLE THEORY OF HEARTACHE

A lma was happy until her routine changed. First there'd been only Mr. Starkhurst to see to. A widower with three grown children who seldom had visitors and ate out a lot was a definite prize. Though the house was large, she had a system of cleaning the rooms in rotation so that each week's duties were fairly light. Granted, hauling the damn vacuum cleaner up those curving stairs was a pain. And carrying the bed linens all the way down to the basement was too, but she tolerated both. Jobs in Dunston didn't grow on trees, as her mother used to say, and she was lucky to have one that not only paid better than most cleaning ladies got (because of her elevated title of "housekeeper," which she'd used during the interview), but also gave her the run of the place. That meant being able to get off her feet at lunch and watch television in the finished basement where she could hear a car in the driveway, or the doorbell, or Mr. Starkhurst unlocking the front door. He never came in by the back door. He said once that when he was growing up his parents insisted that he only come and go that way. The house had once been theirs, and here was Mr. Starkhurst, living in his childhood home, still hurting over some nonsense that happened long ago.

Then Mr. Starkhurst—Chip—took up with Lavinia Dugan. Alma saw right off that she was a brisker wind. In fact Lavinia seemed to freshen the air. Shake up the molecules. Whereas Mr. Starkhurst was set in stone. A major case of opposites attracting.

Chip said, "Lavinia, darling, this is my right arm, this is my Alma."

Alma was in the kitchen. She also cooked. She shoved out her hand in greeting. Her palm was sticky. She forced a smile. Lavinia didn't. She was unhappy that Chip had called her "my Alma," though one look at her said there was nothing to that. Alma was at least fifty, and built like a soup can.

Not long after, Lavinia moved in. Alma thought that each of her children could do with a good smack. They ran around the place like animals. And the noise they made! No more peace and quiet, that was sure. Mr. Starkhurst didn't seem to mind, though, God bless him.

Alma disliked Angie, the eldest, yet felt sorry for her, too. Being overweight like that couldn't be easy. She was pretty enough, but she made herself ugly. Kept her hair chopped short and never put on a speck of makeup. Some women can be pale and quite lovely, Alma thought, remembering her own mother. Angie's pallor was unhealthy and came, Alma was sure, from all the garbage she ate. Alma picked up ten candy wrappers a week from her room. Timothy, the oldest boy, was neat as a pin. Almost obsessive, Alma would say. If she moved his shoes, or set his pencil jar on the other side of the table, it was back in its original place by the end of the day. Alma took to making a little game of it. She'd slide the framed photograph of his father (who looked like one lazy loser to her) a quarter of an inch to the left. Then a half-inch. She wanted to know how much distance would be noticed. Timothy let an inch go by before moving it back. The twin girls wore each other's clothes, switched beds, hairbrushes, even toothbrushes sometimes, so Alma didn't bother trying to keep their belongings properly sorted. And the little one, poor limping Foster, was overrun with stuffed animals. He brought them into bed, leaving barely enough room for himself. In the morning, when he was off at school, Alma found it unnerving to go in and see all those plastic eyes watching her. She was tempted to turn them to the wall, but didn't.

In mid-May Chip announced that his son, Ethan, was coming to visit. Chip's two other children, also sons, lived in Texas. Ethan lived in California. None of the boys had attended Chip's wedding to Lavinia, for the simple reason that they hadn't been asked. Chip explained all this to Lavinia in private. The truth was he didn't want them there. He'd always found it hard being a father, and wasn't very good at reaching out. Lavinia was impressed by his candor. Getting Potter, her ex, to admit he had any failings was like pulling teeth. Chip added that the boys had all been very devoted to their dead mother, which meant they wouldn't have come, even if invited. Lavinia thought that if they couldn't give her a chance, they could go to hell. Life was full of second chances, and who were they to sit in judgment on her and decide, sight unseen, that she wasn't good enough? Wayne and Chip Jr. were in business together. They supplied wholesale plumbing supplies to local contractors and made a bundle. Both were divorced. Neither had children. Ethan was the eldest and clearly the smartest. He got his Ph.D. in physics at the age of twenty-seven from Stanford University, and had taught there for ten years. Lavinia was uneasy to think that she was just six years older than him. His disapproval was sure to be heightened by the age difference between her and his father.

Lavinia made a startling offer. She wanted to handle everything herself during Ethan's visit. Chip didn't understand. She didn't have to demonstrate that she possessed domestic skills, he said. All she had to do was what she did best—be beautiful. His words were light, but they brought instant warmth to her face. She liked being praised. She'd had precious little of it in her life, which was one thing that had attracted her to Chip in the first place. Even so, she wanted to cook her own meals and vacuum her own rugs for a change. She knew it didn't make sense, but she wasn't like some women who always wanted to get out from under housework. She didn't mind it. She never had. Chip was touched. *You're a gem, Lavinia, you really are.* And Alma was given a week off with pay.

Secretly, Lavinia was terrified. Impressing Chip was easy. He'd been lonely when she met him, at loose ends, looking for the next chapter in his life. This unmet son, Ethan, was another story. He was sure to watch every move she made and share his thoughts with his father. Not that Lavinia worried that there'd be any change resulting in Chip's affection. But her esteem was on the line. She needed to show Ethan, and the rest of the world, that Lavinia Dugan Starkhurst was as gracious a hostess as could be found in the whole Finger Lakes region.

Then on the day he was to arrive, she lost steam. She sat in the kitchen with her second-rate pot roast burping to itself on the stove, and lit a cigarette. Who was she kidding? She was a lousy cook. Alma had shown over and over that she could bring flair to the simplest things, like macaroni and cheese. Even her bacon and eggs were outstanding. And as far as making conversation went, she was a flop at that, too. She was out of practice. Maybe she'd never been in practice. Living with Potter didn't make for witty repartee, nor did selling manufactured homes. Chip didn't have much to say, either, so where was she supposed to learn how to be smart and charming?

Lavinia also discovered that she'd forgotten to pick up her favorite blue silk blouse from the dry cleaner's. Her second choice was a lavender suit that she'd worn to the convention in Wilkes-Barre two years before. She credited the suit with her winning the award for most closed sales, that and her proven record of being able to spot a deadbeat. Knowing whom to ask for thirty or more percent down was a rare talent, Chip had said. She decided against the suit. Her attitude worsened. *Screw Chip's son, anyway,* she thought. *What does he think this is, some four-star hotel? He'll take what he gets and damn well like it.* She put on a pair of very tight jeans, high-heeled sandals, a black silk tank top, and a red suede jacket, the kind of thing she might wear to work.

Chip realized he hadn't gone to the liquor store. Lavinia asked what his son drank.

"Beats me. But we're out of Scotch, and unless we want to get through this stone cold sober, I better get going," he said.

Lavinia actually preferred wine, a good French red, but didn't think now was the time to mention that.

Ten minutes later Ethan arrived. The twins let him in. They introduced him to their cats, Tip and Top, who'd been hauled up from the basement to help them open the door. Lavinia came out of the living room and stopped. Ethan finished talking to the twins, then turned to her.

"A vision of loveliness," he said.

"Lavinia."

His teeth were white and even, his jaw perfectly square. He wore a tweed jacket over a tee shirt. He was holding one of the cats, who struggled.

"You better put him down now. He might need to go. Once, my friend was holding him and he had to poop and she didn't know so he just pooped on her," Marta said.

Ethan handed her the cat. "Far be it from me to interfere with the call of nature," he said.

Maggie looked at her sister and shrugged.

"What's for dinner?" she asked Lavinia.

"What? Oh, pot roast. I hope that's all right?"

The question was for Ethan, not the girls.

"I hate pot roast," Marta said.

"Pot roast is one of life's pleasures," Ethan said.

"Take your cats out of here, and tell your brothers to come get Ethan's bag," Lavinia said.

"He's only got one!"

"They can carry it together. Put it in Timothy's room."

"I'm not putting anyone out, am I?" Ethan asked.

"The boys will double up. They're used to it."

"Rough and ready, eh?"

There was that smile again. He needed a shave, she now saw. She hoped he wouldn't shave. It was all right for a man to look a little rugged. Especially when he wore a tweed jacket. It went well together, the stubble and the jacket. He didn't look like a physics professor at all, but a writer, someone who churned out deeply passionate poems that got banned for sexiness.

"Where are my manners? Please, come this way," Lavinia said.

With their footsteps on the tile Lavinia remembered that Ethan had grown up there, and probably knew the place better than she did.

They went into the living room. Ethan stared at the African print over the fireplace. A portrait of his dead mother had once hung there. Lavinia had never seen it. Chip had had the good grace to remove it before her first visit.

"How was your trip?" Lavinia asked.

"Long."

"Yes, I can imagine it was."

Ethan looked around the room slowly. He seemed to see everything in it except her.

"Maybe you can persuade Dad to redecorate. Give the place a more modern feel," he said. He helped himself to a chair. Lavinia sat down, too. She took the end of the sofa nearest him.

"It's a beautiful old house," she said. In fact she hated it. She found it cold and unwelcoming, overly formal. A house should be cozy and make people happy to be in it.

"My great-grandfather had it built in 1923. It was an eyesore, even then. Gaudy and overdone. But he didn't care. He wanted what he wanted."

"And got it."

"Good for him."

Ethan's hostility surprised Lavinia. She wished Chip had given her more to go on. Chip didn't talk much about his children. They seem to have been the main concern of his late wife, and without her, they were of little interest to him. *What will my kids think of me one day?* she suddenly wondered. *What do they think of me now?* She seldom considered whether or not her children liked her as a person, as long as they did what she said. Maybe she should have tried to be better friends with them. Maybe it was still possible, but probably not with Angie. Angie's false accusation of Chip last year had put a hole between them that neither seemed willing to jump over. Lavinia had struggled to understand what lay behind it. Her daughter's heart was a mystery. So was her mean spirit.

"I've upset you," Ethan said.

"What? Oh, no. I was just thinking about something."

"You looked sad."

"Don't be silly."

Shouting voices came from the kitchen, then quieted.

"How many children do you have?" Ethan asked.

"Five."

"Wow. That must have shaken Dad up."

"It did, I'm afraid, but in a good way."

Ethan looked like he didn't believe her. Lavinia felt transparent and as if anything she said would sound false.

"I'm glad he finally invited you to come," she said.

"It was my idea. Guess I got curious to see what you were really like."

"I hope I'll meet with your approval."

Chip returned with the liquor. Lavinia was surprised by the warm hug and back thumps the two men exchanged. Chip was positively grinning, and so was Ethan. She felt left out. She wanted to catch Ethan's eye and remind him that she was still there. Then Chip sat down, put his arm around her, and asked Ethan what he thought of his new little wife. When Ethan looked at her then, his eyes seemed cold, and she wasn't glad at all.

When she couldn't sleep, Lavinia padded along the carpeted upstairs hall to check on the children. A light was visible beneath Ethan's door, even as late as two a.m. In the morning, when the children were off to school, he was at the table with the paper. Lavinia went to make up his room before she left for work. There was always a book by his bed, a novel or volume of poetry. She tried to imagine him lying there, reading. In the raw, too, since she never found any pajamas, shorts, or even an old tee shirt. He was divorced. Chip had given some details. His former daughter-in-law had been "flighty," spent too much money, wasn't content to live on a professor's salary. After the break-up, Chip sensed a deep change in Ethan. He was bitter, and refused to let it show. That was almost nine years ago. The trouble between them—Chip and Ethan—was that Chip had never liked the woman and thought from the outset that Ethan was making a mistake. "A youthful rebellion," Chip called it. Chip felt that Ethan's wanting to come east now proved that he'd turn a crucial corner and was ready to accept that his father had had only his best interests at heart.

Lavinia sensed that Ethan was still heart sore over his divorce. Maybe there'd been another relationship after the ex-wife that ended badly, too. Maybe several. He was often quiet and lost in thought. Sometimes he wandered from room to room, as if to recall his own childhood, and the boy he'd once been. Or maybe he was just bored and had decided that his visit was a waste of time. Lavinia wished she knew the truth, whatever it was.

The children were indifferent to Ethan, except Angie, who thought he was drop-dead gorgeous. That such a fine specimen could be related to Chip was hard to fathom. She kept her thoughts on Ethan to herself. She knew her brothers and sisters would take any chance to make her miserable by teasing her, if they could, and the only way to stop that would be to get physical. Lavinia had forbidden all hitting, slapping, pinching, hair pulling, and kicking. Angie could still spit, she supposed. She could hawk a loogie as well as anyone. What the other children noticed was that Ethan bothered their mother. She stopped talking whenever he came into the room, and stayed quiet while he was there. At dinner she didn't look at him, which must have been awkward, since he'd taken the empty chair directly across from her. They assumed that she was falling prey to her usual sense of superiority. She shut out people she looked down on. Though it was hard to look down on Ethan. He was very smart. His first night there, he'd explained about Einstein's theory of relativity in simple terms. Foster, the brightest, understood it immediately. It worried him to think that the universe was expanding, because Foster tended to worry about a lot of things, especially those he couldn't control, and Ethan quietly said that the expansion was very, very slow, and that when Foster was an old man, the change in distance would be impossible to see. Angie thought it was Ethan's voice more than his words that put Foster at ease. At the mention of relative time, the twins talked about time travel because they'd just seen a science fiction movie where people jumped back and forth through the ages, and they decided that one day they wanted to go back to a medieval castle and be princesses.

"You'd get the plague," Timothy said. His history class had just covered that same topic.

"What's that?" Marta asked.

"An illness spread by fleas biting people," Ethan said. "Caused a severe inflammatory response, which accounted for the black boils observed on the bodies of the sick."

Chip put down his fork and stared at Ethan. The others couldn't tell if he was proud of Ethan's knowledge or disgusted by what he'd heard. Lavinia changed the subject and talked about the warm spring weather, and how she hoped her garden would do better than it had the year before. Angie hoped she wasn't boring Ethan stiff. He smiled and nodded and looked like someone trying very hard not to laugh.

The weekend came, and with it the final two days of Ethan's visit. For the first time, Lavinia found the house confining, all fifty-three hundred square feet of it. She organized a picnic at the lake. The twins had gone on a sleepover, and Chip had a golf came he couldn't get out of with the president of a bank he was on the board of. She asked Angie to help her make sandwiches. Angie would have refused under different circumstances, but knowing that one would be eaten by Ethan was enough to make her get to work. Ethan came in for a cup of coffee and offered to help. Lavinia asked him how he felt about hard-boiled eggs, and Angie wanted to crawl under the table because that didn't seem like the kind of thing you asked a man with a brain like Ethan's.

"Good for snacking, or pitching at rowdies," he said. Angie was surprised. Rowdies? Another layer of Ethan had revealed itself.

Lavinia said nothing. She went on cracking and peeling the eggs one by one. Ethan took an egg from the bowl and peeled it, too. Angie made seven bologna sandwiches, five with peanut butter and jelly, and one with just salami. All the while, Lavinia and Ethan peeled eggs silently. Angie couldn't find a reason to stay in the kitchen any longer, so she left. She looked back to see her mother and Ethan standing side by side, their hands moving, their faces still, as if they'd be executed on the spot if they stopped for one second.

Angie didn't like going to the lake and never had. Today she thought the water was too cold. Timothy and Foster didn't mind it, though they quickly got tired of swimming. Timothy found a girl he knew from school and moved his stuff over to where she was sitting with two other friends, which left Angie to keep Foster amused. He was soon bored, so Lavinia suggested taking him up the trail to the falls. Angie didn't want to and saw that there was no choice. Foster was getting fussy and wound up and needed to spend his energy, like a dog, she often thought. They put on their shoes and at Lavinia's command, a thick layer of sunblock that the water had washed off. Angie thought of the fish somewhere out in the lake, gagging on sunblock and kid pee. If people really wanted to clean up the planet, a good place to start would be keeping kids out of the lake.

Lavinia sat on a towel beneath a large striped umbrella. She didn't like being in direct sun. Ethan was used to it, living in California. He lay beside her in a pair of old swim trunks Chip had lent him which were too big in the waist. He'd had to use a safety pin to gather them up in the back. Lavinia had helped him do it. She remembered that now, how she'd stood right behind him while he had his shirt off. She was in an Indian print skirt with a gold hem and a white tank top. She worried that the outfit was too young for her, especially given how critically Angie had looked at her as they were getting in the car.

The water was cut by wavy arcs of light. An old woman in a white one-piece suit picked her way along the stony shore. The flesh on her arms and legs sagged. Knotted blue veins bulged on her calves and thighs. Lavinia hated the idea of growing old. At forty-three, she liked to think she could pass for thirty-five, someone nearer Ethan's age, someone he might even date.

She wondered if people seeing them assumed that they were a couple. Not a new couple, maybe, because they didn't touch, but one that had been together for a while and gotten comfortable not talking. A happily married couple with no children. People who lived a civilized life where they traveled, read interesting books, and had kind, wise friends.

She imagined that a professor's life was an easy one. You got every summer off. You got to travel to conferences and meetings, and present papers or whatever it was you did. And everyone respected you because you were educated.

"So, you leave us tomorrow," she said.

"Yes."

"Have you enjoyed your visit?"

"Very much."

"Was it hard getting time off from teaching?"

"I had the whole semester off."

"Really, why?"

"Sabbatical."

"Oh."

Lavinia didn't know what that was, and Ethan didn't explain.

"What will you do this summer?" she asked. She wondered how much longer it would be before Angie and Foster returned.

"Don't know yet. Might teach a session, though I don't usually like to. Students aren't quite as serious in the summer. Either that, or they're too serious, because they're trying not to flunk out. Sometimes they pressure you."

There was a tension in his voice that suggested his firsthand experience with this had been both unpleasant and fairly recent.

A female student had thrown herself at him, Lavinia decided. He was probably used to it, yet it still bothered him. He seemed like the kind of man who wouldn't take advantage of a thing like that, as some might.

He was looking at her and she'd only just noticed. She blushed. He smiled at her.

"Lie next to me, and we'll watch the clouds. You can tell me what you see," he said. The sun had moved towards the western shore. A willow tree was now casting broken shade on the sand. She lay down next to him and watched the sky through her sunglasses. He looked up, too. The clouds were swift, now that the wind had picked up. Neither of them spoke. When his hand brushed hers, she flinched.

"Sorry," he said.

"It's okay."

"A train."

"What?"

"That one's like a train, don't you think?"

"Yes."

Lavinia wasn't looking at the clouds. Her eyes were closed. A tear ran down her cheek. She didn't brush it away.

"It's a long way away," she said.

"What is?"

"California."

"Only five hours by plane."

"Are you happy there?"

"Not always."

Ethan said she was welcome to visit any time. She could even bring the kids. He didn't mention Chip. Neither did Lavinia. A door opened within her, daring her to step through. She did.

"You'd just end up hating yourself," Ethan said.

Just then, Foster and Angie appeared. Foster said he was hungry. Ethan and Foster went to the car to get the cooler out of the trunk, and Angie and Lavinia gathered their things and set off to find an empty picnic table.

Had to catch an earlier flight, didn't want to wake you. Thanks for everything. Love, Ethan. The note was propped up against the china sugar bowl in the kitchen. Lavinia had gotten up at six-thirty so she could see him off. She sat down on one of the stools. She was still sitting there when Chip came down an hour later.

"Oh, that's Ethan all over. When he's ready to go, he's gone, even if it means changing his plans," he said.

"I didn't know he'd changed his plans."

"I heard him making the call yesterday. I forgot to tell you. You're not disappointed, I hope."

"It would have been nice to say good-bye."

The night before, they took him out to dinner at Madeline's. The children had come, too. It was festive and happy, and all the time Ethan sat right next to her, knowing it was the last time she'd see him and not saying anything. The blue silk blouse had come back from the cleaners and she worn it. She looked great, she knew that much, but getting Ethan to even look at her had been difficult.

"Are you all right?" Chip asked. He'd settled down across from her with the newspaper.

"Yes."

"Why don't you go in a little late today? You look tired."

"Can't. Got those clients coming in from Elmira."

"Refresh my memory."

"Wanted to buy at least three or four homes. Runs a trailer park over there, and he wants to upgrade."

"You're the girl to help him do it, too."

But Lavinia changed her mind and called in sick after Chip went to play another game of golf. Alma found her in Timothy's room, sound asleep in her bathrobe. Her face was still wet from crying. She looked so pathetic, Alma thought, like a little girl. She debated whether or not to wake her, and decided to leave her be. It was hard enough having a fight with your husband, especially when he'd kicked you out for the night, and you had to ask your own son to give up his bed for you. It would blow over soon enough, Alma was sure. The house was in good shape, nice and clean, all the laundry done. Mr. Starkhurst would forgive Lavinia for whatever it was, Alma thought, once he realized how hard she'd worked in her absence.

INTO MY LOVING ARMS

To celebrate not flunking out of high school and actually making it to graduation, Angie Dugan asked for a small necklace she'd found at the Pyramid Mall off of Route 13. It was a simple serpentine chain in fourteen karat gold, with silver balls about an inch apart. The necklace was a bit short for Angie's neck. Angie's friend Luann pointed that out when Angie tried it on. Luann said something to the effect that the necklace made Angie look like a dog straining at the leash. Angie didn't care. It was pretty and she wanted it. That was all. Luann said the necklace was nice, but wouldn't Angie prefer cash? Angie's stepfather, Chip Starkhurst, was loaded. With an opportunity like that, cash only made sense.

Angie was to receive neither the necklace nor cash. She was being given a barbecue by the lake. She didn't want a barbecue by the lake. Barbecues sucked. So did the lake. But what Angie wanted was immaterial. Her parents—divorced three years by then—had made the decision for her.

It was her father's idea. He believed in simple pleasures, like watching sunsets, counting sailboats on the water, and whiskey. Not necessarily in that order. In making the suggestion, he knew he'd have to spend time with his ex-wife's new husband, something he didn't look forward to. Lavinia, the ex-wife, didn't think it was a good idea to put the two men together. But since any sort of celebration would have to include both of them, she put aside her concerns and got busy. It was assumed that she would make all the arrangements, like reserving the shelter, and planning the menu. Potter said he'd provide the beverages.

Added to Lavinia's woe—and Angie's, too—was that Potter's sister Patty and her boyfriend Murph were coming out from Montana for the occasion. Lavinia and Patty didn't see eye to eye on anything, but that wasn't the problem. When Angie had spent time with Patty and Murph two summers before, there'd been some trouble, unspecified trouble because Patty agreed to keep her mouth shut in exchange for putting Angie on the next bus back to Dunston. Lavinia figured Patty had done something to piss Angie off. Potter figured that too and didn't say so, because he was generally very fond of his sister and owed her a lot. Only Patty, Murph, and Angie knew the truth, which was that Angie had offered to give Murph a blow job one day when they'd been alone in his truck.

Since then, Angie had had to ask herself some hard questions, like what the hell she had been thinking. The moment the words came out of her mouth she was terrified that Murph might actually take her up on it. She'd never engaged in oral sex before and knew it was something she'd never have the guts to try.

"You were fucked up in the head," Luann said. "When you're fucked up in the head, you do crazy things."

That craziness began about a month before going west. Angie came out of her bathroom and stubbed her toe on the foot of her French provincial dresser. She quickly made her displeasure known. Chip was going down the hall, reflecting on his most recent golf game where he'd scored a dramatic three under par. He wasn't used to such success on the green. Nor was he used to sudden shrieks. He assumed the worst and rushed to the rescue. Angie was in her bathrobe, but she hadn't fastened it.

"So he saw your tits," Luann said.

"Yup."

"Must have freaked the bastard out."

Chip turned red, coughed, said something, and left.

Angie's brother, Timothy, saw Chip leave her room, then walked in without knocking and demanded to know what had gone on. Angie

76

didn't enlighten him. In fact, she didn't enlighten anyone, and in her detached state of mind, found it fascinating to see how quickly everyone assumed the worst. Her mother thought she should stay with her father for a while, which she did. But Potter, though loving and kind, was a bore, and Angie got restless. It was at that point that she was packed off to Montana.

Luann invited herself to the barbecue. Her own parents hadn't planned anything in her honor. They were busy people. Her father was a dentist and her mother sold real estate, and after watching her walk across the stage to get her diploma, they planned to go out to dinner. Alone. When Angie told her mother that Luann was coming, she sighed. Potter had asked to bring someone, too.

"Yeah, who?" Angie asked.

"How should I know? Probably that fool he goes bowling with, Rodney what's-his-name."

One reason her parents never got along was that her mother hated all of her father's friends. Lavinia hated just about everyone, Angie decided. In fact, she was hard pressed to name someone her mother actually liked. Even Chip wore thin from time to time. Lavinia seemed to tolerate him more than she loved him. The only one she ever mentioned with the slightest fondness was Ethan, Chip's son, who'd come to visit from California the year before. There'd been some talk of the family all going to see him there, but that fell through. Angie assumed that Ethan had come to his senses and realized that being descended upon by his father and six Dugans—or former Dugans, in her mother's case—was a really bad idea. Lavinia had contacted Ethan to invite him to Angie's event on the grounds that he and Angie had formed a bond during his stay. Ethan begged off. He'd send a gift, he promised. So far, nothing had arrived.

Patty and Murph had car trouble in Indiana, but managed to reach Dunston two days before the barbecue. Patty had assumed that they'd stay with Potter. Something came up at the last minute, and they were diverted to Chip's house instead. Potter was probably on a bender,

Patty explained to Murph. A bender sounded fine to him. He was nervous being in new territory, hanging out in a rich guy's house where Lavinia, about whom he'd heard nothing good, might as well wear a whistle around her neck, the way she gave orders. She and Patty were very much alike in that respect, which probably accounted for why they didn't get along. It was Murph's experience that when two women of the same outlook on life (bitchy) got together, sparks flew.

On their first night in town, Potter took Murph out for drinks. Patty begged off. She was tired. Later Angie came into her bedroom— Timothy's, once again—and said she was glad she'd come.

"Nice of you to say," Patty said. She was laying out the few things she'd brought on the bed, trying to decide what to wear the following day. June in Dunston could still be iffy, and there was a chance of rain. She'd included a thick white sweater that she could put over her favorite sundress, but that way she'd look like a polar bear. Probably better just to freeze, in that case.

"Where's Murph?" Angie asked.

Patty gave her a long, cool stare. "Out getting loaded with your dad. Why?"

"Just wanted to say hello."

"Come back later, assuming he's in any shape to be sociable."

Murph staggered in after everyone had gone to bed. The next morning Chip found him in his study wearing a wife-beater, plaid boxer shorts, and a pair of yellow flip-flops. Murph was helping himself to a small glass of single-malt scotch from Chip's sideboard.

"Hair of the dog," Murph said. "Hope you don't mind."

"Not at all. Chip Starkhurst. Sorry we didn't get a chance to meet last night." Chip had had another of his board meetings, announced at the last minute, and Lavinia decided he wanted to put off meeting more members of her extended family for as long as he could.

"Hell of a place you got here," Murph said.

"It's old and cranky. Like me. Lavinia wants me to sell it and buy a brand new house."

"Old houses got their own charm. I grew up in one. Great place, until the roof caved in one winter."

Chip drank from the ceramic coffee mug in his hand. It said *Kiss Me, I'm Polish* in red script letters. Murph didn't think Chip looked Polish, but then he had no idea what a Polish person looked like.

Chip told Murph to pour a shot of scotch into his coffee.

Murph obliged. "Nothing like an Irish Whiskey to get the day on its feet," he said.

Chip invited Murph to sit on one of the leather couches. Murph sat.

"What do you do in Montana?" Chip asked.

"The usual. Work, when I can get it, which isn't too often. Landscaping, moving, light hauling, that sort of thing."

"Your wife's in the restaurant business."

"You're only half right. She's the manager for the Dusty Boot, but she's not my wife."

"Never asked her?"

"Once. After I'd had a few."

Chip laughed. The sound echoed off the tile hallway beyond the open door. Chip led Murph into the kitchen, where Alma was scrambling eggs. Alma took in Murph's outfit with narrow eyes, then set two places at the wooden kitchen table.

Patty appeared, wearing a huge Green Bay Packers tee shirt. Her hair was matted. She drank coffee and ate a small piece of toast in silence. Then Lavinia came in, looking rested, with an angry gleam in her eye, which meant that she felt there was still too much to do to get ready for the barbecue. She leaned over the kitchen sink and looked through the window at the sky, hoping it was still clear. Murph admired her ass. Chip saw him and laughed again.

"What's so funny?" Lavinia asked. Her tone was sharp.

"The ways of man," Chip said.

"Uh, huh." Lavinia looked at Chip, then at Murph.

"You're drinking. At this time of day," she said to Chip.

Chip lifted his mug as if to toast her.

All three women stared at Murph, who took a minute to notice.

"Don't look at me. It was his idea," Murph said.

Lavinia saw what she'd planned for the day disintegrate. Patty must have seen it, too, because she got up, took Murph's glass and Chip's coffee mug to the sink, and poured them both out.

"Plenty of time for that later, for God's sake," she said. "Now finish your breakfast and help Lavinia get this show on the road." Patty pinched Murph's ear on her way out of the kitchen. Murph squawked. Alma grinned. *There's a Dunston girl,* she thought. Hard-edged and honest as a line.

Chip watched Patty go, too. The way she favored one leg reminded him of Foster. Maybe it was a family trait. But whether they walked on two good legs or not, they were nothing you'd get around. Nothing you'd want to get around. Maybe that's why Lavinia had pulled herself away. Cutting your own path across that tribe wouldn't be easy.

As if she read his mind, Lavinia stood with crossed arms. She'd gone back to wearing jumpsuits. This one was green. She wore a gold chain around her neck. As she ran down her mental list of chores, her fingers played with it, and it was then that she remembered what Angie had asked her for as a gift.

For the moment the weather was cooperating. The trees along the bank swayed in a gentle onshore breeze. Even so, Lavinia wanted to secure the tablecloth with four smooth round stones she'd instructed Foster and the twins to find at the water's edge and bring back. There was algae on them, which meant they had to be rinsed, and that meant finding an in-ground faucet. Foster didn't see why they couldn't be washed in the lake itself, and both Marta and Maggie called him a moron.

"The lake's full of goose shit," Maggie said. She was wearing a yellow hairband that matched both her top and pants. Marta was identically dressed, only her ensemble was green, like Lavinia's jumpsuit.

"So what? It won't get in our food," Foster said.

INTO MY LOVING ARMS

"It might, and then what?" Angie asked. She wore her usual denim coveralls with a black tank top underneath. It was about one-thirty, or maybe two, and she was already having a lousy time.

The children, including Timothy who was eating pretzels from a bag his mother had ordered him not to touch, went off and sat under the shade of a tall tree. A deck of cards was pulled out. Soon Go Fish was in full swing. Patty and Murph washed the rocks, then laid them out exactly as Lavinia had instructed. Patty stood back and regarded their handiwork. Murph thought she looked cute. She'd decided against her dress and gone for a plaid short-sleeved shirt and torn blue jeans. He was proud of her, of how western they both looked. He'd put on his denim shirt, the one with the mother-of-pearl buttons, and a bolo tie with a big turquoise stone. He wondered if the sky over the lake was the same color as the sky back home. He removed his tie and lifted it up to compare.

"Whatcha got there?" Chip asked. He had a cup in his hand. He'd brought along the scotch from his den and had been drinking slowly but steadily.

"Just seeing how things line up," Murph said.

"Yeah? What things?"

Murph explained. Chip was enthralled. He'd never been further than Ohio, he said. Always thought the West was full of lowlife cretins.

"No offense," Chip said. He'd spilled liquor on the front of his knit sweater. His neck was red, and his teeth were even and too white. Dentures probably, Murph figured.

"None taken. You're not far off. Some folks out there are as dumb as wood," Murph said and put his tie back on.

Chip laughed so hard he bent over in the middle. Murph caught Patty's eye. She was at the grill with Lavinia, coaxing up the fire they'd just lit.

"Yo, Chip! Why don't you come and have a nice cold glass of lemonade?" Patty asked. She was used to this sort of thing. The Dusty Boot was a family restaurant, except late at night when it wasn't. She'd wrestled her fair share of drunks out the door. Patty was small, but wiry. If you crossed her, she'd shove you right on your ass.

Chip didn't want any lemonade, but said he wouldn't mind taking a load off his feet. Patty guided him into a lawn chair set up in the shade. She covered him with a thin blanket. Patty was amused that Chip couldn't hold his liquor. Lavinia clearly wasn't. Patty could tell she blamed Murph, as if Chip were some teenager he'd bought beer for, not an adult who made his own decisions. *Well, too bad about that,* Patty thought. She wasn't about to start caring what Lavinia thought.

Soon the fire was almost ready, and Lavinia didn't know if she should start grilling. Potter wasn't there yet. She asked Patty her opinion.

"Well, he knows what time we wanted to eat, and he knows how to tell time, so if he's not here, that's his tough luck," Patty said. Chip's eyes were shut. A leaf had fallen into his lap.

Lavinia started slapping the burgers together in a way that suggested she'd rather be slapping someone's face. Patty didn't think it was healthy to have all that anger inside all the time. She helped by setting the table.

Potter arrived in a car no one recognized. A woman got out of the passenger side. She was short and round, like a meatball. There was a child in the back seat, and the woman helped her with the door. The child's eyes were too small, and her jaw was slack. Down syndrome, Patty figured. The woman had a brown grocery bag, which she put on the table. She took four bottles of cheap wine out of the bag, and a bottle of gin. At the very bottom she found a corkscrew.

"Thank god. Didn't want to leave that behind," she said.

"Cici Sloan. Good heavens," Lavinia said.

Cici took Lavinia in with a cool, critical look.

"Lavinia. You look just the same, after all this time," she said.

"When did you guys hang out?" Potter asked.

"We didn't. But we had gym together in ninth grade," Cici said.

"Not gym. American History," Lavinia said.

The little girl was tugging at Cici's hand and grunting.

"Stop it," Cici said. The child went on with her tugging. She tried to twist out of Cici's grasp.

"Oh, by the way, this is Annabelle," Cici said to Lavinia and Potter. "She's my daughter's third kid."

Lavinia digested the fact that Cici was a grandmother. It figured. The Sloans were always trashy. Cici's daughter probably started pushing them out when she was fifteen, if family history held true. Cici had had to leave school then because she was pregnant. She'd had a boy who was later killed in a car wreck. He'd been driving without a license. The paper said he was only thirteen. Lavinia didn't know she'd had a daughter, but then why would she? She hadn't seen Cici once in all those years.

Potter saw the scotch Chip had brought and poured himself a cup. Then he asked what he could do to help.

"Just stay out of the way," Lavinia said.

Patty introduced herself and Murph to Cici. Cici appraised Murph in a slow, lusty glance.

"Nice tie," she told him.

"Thanks."

Potter called his children over to meet Cici and Annabelle. Their heads turned, then turned back. He called again. They got up slowly, and sauntered barefoot through the grass.

Angie stared at Annabelle.

"What's wrong with her?" Marta asked.

"Retarded," Cici said. "But she does all right, don't you Annabelle?"

"All. Right." Annabelle's voice was deep and thick.

"She's sweet. Does she want a popsicle?" Maggie asked. "We only have orange."

Annabelle nodded.

"I ate the last one," Timothy said.

"Asshole."

"Maggie, please do not use that kind of language," Lavinia said.

"Take Annabelle over to the 7-Eleven and get her a popsicle. And anything else you want."

"It's all the way across the road!"

"That makes it less than a half-mile. Won't kill you," Potter said. He brought out his wallet and handed Angie a twenty-dollar bill. Everyone, including Cici, wondered where he'd gotten it. Potter said he was pretty broke, which is why they'd taken her car.

The children moved off. Angie had Annabelle by the hand. Potter joined Murph at the table. Cici sat, too. Patty set out the ketchup and mustard, then unwrapped a package of sliced American cheese. In her restaurant, they never served American cheese on their burgers. Only cheddar.

After a while, Angie's friend Luann arrived on her bicycle. Her face was sweaty from her ride. She was a tall girl, with strong arms and legs, and not a bit of fat.

"You rode all that way?" Patty asked. It was over seven miles from town.

"Sure. Do it all the time."

"Your timing's good. They just went over to the store. You bring it?"

"Right here."

Luann had the necklace Angie wanted. Patty had arranged it. Luann was at the house when she and Murph arrived, and Patty stopped her on her way out and asked if she knew what Angie was getting for graduation. She'd struggled with herself a little before giving Luann the money to buy it. She still thought Angie was a big fat skunk for what she'd done back in Helena, but she could tell that she was trying to smooth it over, and probably deserved the chance.

"Nice," said Murph.

"What's that?" Lavinia asked.

"Angie's present."

"Oh, I see."

"Graduating's a big deal. Didn't want to just give a gift card, or something dumb like that," Patty said.

"Right."

"What's she going to do next year, by the way? I didn't ask her yet."

"She applied to SUNY Cortland and got wait-listed. Her grades weren't exactly stellar."

Chip opened his eyes and asked what time it was. No one answered him. Patty held the necklace up for another look.

"Oh, it's just like yours. That's why she must have wanted it," Patty said to Lavinia. A flush of color rose in Lavinia's cheeks.

"You bring the wrapping paper?" Luann asked.

"Hot pink. And the scotch tape, too," Patty said.

"Here, let me."

Luann worked fast. She creased the paper perfectly, so it lay smooth and flat.

"Ta-da," she said.

"Needs a bow," Cici said.

"She's right," Murph said.

"Well, we don't have one," Patty said.

"Kids aren't back yet. We can shoot into town."

"Too far."

"Come on. I want some potato salad," Murph said.

Lavinia was peeved. She'd expressly omitted potato salad because it was so messy.

"Oh, all right. If they get back before we do, go ahead and start without us," Patty said. She and Murph got in his truck and pulled away. Luann went off to find Angie at the store.

Lavinia sat down. She asked Cici if she'd mind opening one of the bottles of wine she'd brought. Cici had thoughtfully supplied both red and white. She asked Lavinia which one she preferred. Lavinia said red.

Potter watched her take the plastic cup from Cici, look into it, and then drink. Her lips were pulled down, and her brows had come together. He knew that expression. He'd seen it a lot. He asked Cici to go back to the car and get his jacket, because he thought he'd want it later. Cici said he'd be fine without it. He asked her again. She sighed. She opened a bottle of white wine, poured herself a huge cup, and took it with her.

"What's eating you?" he asked Lavinia, once they were alone.

"Nothing."

"Bull."

Chip snored in his chair. He listed to one side, like a dingy taking on water.

"Come on. Something's got you all uptight. Just tell me what it is," Potter said.

Lavinia gently shook her cup so that the wine sloshed back and forth. Then she put the cup on the table, and put her hands in her lap. She pushed the hair that escaped her fancy silver clip back behind her ear.

"I should have gotten her the necklace. She told me she wanted it, and I didn't think it was an appropriate gift," she said.

"Why not? Afraid she'd hock it?"

"Shut up, Potter."

"All right, but why did you think she shouldn't have it?"

For trying to pull a fast one, and make everyone think Chip did what he hadn't done.

"Why are you crying?" Potter asked.

"She's not a bad girl."

"Of course she's not."

"She just can't figure the odds."

Potter considered this. He had no idea what she was talking about. He gave her another cup of wine. Cici hadn't come back with the jacket yet. She probably assumed they were having an argument and wanted to steer clear.

Lavinia wiped her nose on her lime-colored sleeve. Angie's eyes had been full of light when she asked for the necklace. After everything that had happened, she really believed that Lavinia would say yes. Because that's what mothers were supposed to do—let their kids off the hook.

"She's worth it, isn't she?" Lavinia asked.

"Who? Angie?"

"Who else?"

That was just like Potter to miss the point. Their daughter had done wrong and needed to be forgiven.

I'm no good at that. She'd never felt she could afford to be. She'd spent her whole life being as hard and straight as a brick. Well, bricks built things, but they could break them, too.

"Potter?"

"Yes?"

"Have you ever forgiven me?"

"For leaving?"

Lavinia nodded.

"I figured you just didn't love me enough," Potter said.

"I loved you enough."

"Well, then."

He put his hand on hers and she grabbed it hard. It hurt. His heart quickened. He didn't want this to happen. He didn't want the complication.

Lavinia looked into his face and he was pulled back to their early days. Such passion she had in her then. How her jaw could be straight, and then go all quivery touched him so. God, how he'd loved her! And where had it all gone? He still had love in him, he knew that. Cici was trying hard to pry out what was left. Maybe one day he'd feel for her what he'd once felt for Lavinia. But right now, with Lavinia's hand bearing down on his, that day was slipping away.

Lavinia released his hand. She looked at the cup in front of her.

"Not exactly a superior vintage, is it?" she asked.

"Cici's no expert."

"Where did you meet her?"

"The Laundromat."

"The washer die again?"

"It was never too lively."

Lavinia remembered that rental house. It used to drive her nuts, the way nothing worked right. She knew deep down that her new life with Chip wasn't exactly the one she wanted, but she also knew that she'd reached a point where having things that didn't break was pretty damn important.

"Is it serious?" Lavinia asked.

"The washer?"

"Cici."

"She wants to get married."

"What about you?"

Potter shrugged. "I guess I'm for it."

"Beats being alone, right?"

"Sometimes."

Lavinia laughed. Potter hit the mark on that one.

Cici tossed Potter's jacket on the far end of the table. She sat down there, too, to express her irritation. The children returned with the snacks they'd bought already eaten, except for Annabelle, who was still slurping her popsicle. She had an orange stain around her mouth and down the hand that was clutching the stick. The front of her pink coveralls were dirty, too. She toddled over to where Chip still sat in his lawn chair and stared at him. Then she poked his cheek.

He opened his eyes. "Hello," he said.

Annabelle said nothing, turned away, and went back to Angie. She shoved her whole body up against Angie's thigh.

Cici was on her third round of wine, and when she saw Annabelle called out, "Hey, girl, get your ass over here!"

Annabelle went on hugging Angie.

Potter said, "Keep your cool, for God's sake. This is supposed to be a party."

Cici tapped the tip of Potter's nose with her cup.

Patty and Murph came back with two gallons of potato salad and a twelve-pack of beer. Murph figured it was time to switch over from scotch and slow down a little. He strode over the lawn, tore a beer out of the cardboard box, and offered one to Chip as he struggled to his feet.

"Not for me, thanks," Chip said.

Chip felt foggy, but content. The alcohol had relaxed him, and so had his nap. He joined the group already at table. He looked at the faces around him. Everyone seemed content, too, except Lavinia. He wished she'd learn to lighten up.

Angie sat with Annabelle across from Cici.

"How old is she?" Angie asked her.

"Huh? Her? Uh, four. No, five."

"Can she feed herself?"

"Sure. But she's a wicked slob."

Angie cut Annabelle's hamburger into four small pieces and tied a cloth dishtowel around her neck. Annabelle hummed while she ate, and swung her legs, which made the whole bench jiggle.

Cici asked her to stop. Annabelle didn't stop.

"Hey, girl, stop that bumping around. You're messing up everyone's meal here."

Angie stared at Cici and hoped she'd get the message. She didn't. Foster put down his plastic fork. Foster had a sixth sense. Cici reached across the table and smacked Annabelle in the face hard enough to send the food out of her mouth and onto Angie's plate. Silence fell. Annabelle wailed. Her face turned red and scrunched up like a newborn's. Potter got to his feet and put his hands on Cici's shoulders. He thought she might be ready to hand out a few more blows. Angie lifted Annabelle's cup of lemonade and tossed it into Cici's face.

Patty shouted, "You go, girl!" Timothy clapped. Marta and Maggie giggled. Foster looked desperately at his mother, whose face was white.

"You fucking bitch!" Cici screamed, and tried to get to her feet. Potter let her, then got her by the arm and steered her across the lawn towards the far end of the parking lot. Cici struggled against his grip and went on yelling. A small group of people formed to watch.

"My goodness," Chip said.

"He should have cut that one off a while ago," Murph said. He kept eating. He thought the potato salad was particularly tasty, and just the way he liked it, with a good serving of mustard mixed in.

Angie wiped Annabelle off and tried to soothe her. The twins offered some candy they'd brought from home. Annabelle accepted a Tootsie roll. Timothy poured her another glass of lemonade.

"My goodness," Chip said again.

Lavinia's lower lip was trembling. She'd known all along that sooner or later the day would go to hell.

Luann, who'd been in the bathroom the whole time, returned and asked, "What happened?"

"You missed a brawl," Murph said. Lavinia wiped her eyes. Chip poured her another cup of wine. Annabelle sucked her Tootsie roll, hummed, and swung her legs. She looked up at Angie and smiled. Angie kissed her on the top of her head. She smelled greasy, as if her hair hadn't been washed for a while.

They could all hear Cici's voice, but not her words. She was waving her arms. She lurched back towards the shelter more than once, and each time Potter restrained her. Then she tried to hit him, and he stepped out of her way. She lost her balance and fell. Potter helped her up. She was still shouting.

The crowd watching them grew.

"That one needs a dunk lakeside," Angie said. The thought of Cici flailing in the water amused her.

"Uh, oh," Luann said.

A police car that had been patrolling the parking lot pulled up to where Potter still had ahold of Cici. Murph immediately stopped eating. He hated cops. Patty stood up.

"Oh, god! She'll say he did something to her unless we get our asses over there quick," she said.

Everyone left the table and made for the parking lot except Lavinia and Chip. Lavinia put her face in her hands. Chip patted her back. His burger was cold and he wondered how long he'd have to wait before asking her to put another one on the grill for him.

"It's not your fault," he told her.

"I know it's not. I just wanted this to be a nice day for everyone."

"Well, they'll probably take Cici home, and then things will improve."

"I can't believe how hard she hit that kid."

"A first for me, I have to say."

In the parking lot, with two very young officers trying to ask questions, Cici was crying hysterically.

"Too much wine," Potter said. "I thought she needed to take a little walk, you know."

The blond officer nodded. His hair resembled the bristles on a shoe brush.

"You folks all out here together?" the red-haired officer asked.

"It's my graduation party," Angie said. She was holding Annabelle in her arms.

"I'm sorry," Cici said. "I'm sorry." She had dust on her pants from falling down. She brushed herself off, which caused her to teeter.

"It's okay, honey. We all overdo it sometimes," Potter said.

The children realized that no one was going to say what had happened unless Cici spoke up first. If she accused Angie of anything, they'd all say she'd smacked Annabelle. That would get her arrested in no time.

Annabelle whined and Angie put her down. She trotted back towards the picnic shelter, and Angie went after her. The officers soon agreed that Cici had had too much to drink, gotten out of control, and should just go on home.

"My thoughts exactly. I'll get right on that," Potter said.

"What about, what about –" Cici said.

"Don't worry. We'll bring her home. Let her stay and enjoy herself a little longer," Potter said. Cici was like a balloon that had leaked out all its air. Her arms looked like they didn't know how to hang off her body.

"Tell your mom I'll be back," Potter told Timothy.

"Why don't you let me drive?" Patty asked.

Potter nodded. "Maybe you ought," he said.

"I'll get my pack."

"Leave the present on the table," he whispered to her. Patty nodded.

After Potter, Cici, and Patty left, Murph and the four remaining children started walking slowly back.

"She was really loaded," Maggie said.

"Drunker than a skunk," Marta said.

"Three sheets to the wind," Foster said.

Murph figured that they must have learned those phrases listening to their mother chew out their father.

"She didn't have that much. Not as far as I could see," Timothy said.

"She's a small woman. Doesn't take a lot in a body that size," Murph said.

"I want a Coke," Foster said.

"Me, too," Maggie said.

"You guys have any money?" Murph asked.

"Some," Marta said.

"All right, let's make a little detour."

When they returned to the shelter, Angie and Annabelle were in the lawn chair Chip had napped in before. Now it was Annabelle who was sound asleep, her fingers laced through Angie's. Around Annabelle's neck was Angie's new gold chain.

"She saw the present on the table and thought it was for her," Angie said, in a voice quiet enough to keep Annabelle from waking.

"Are you going to let her keep it?" Foster asked.

"I don't know."

She already decided she would, though. And from the way she cradled Annabelle there in the chair, everyone else knew it, too.

MAGGIE'S DARE

When they were very young, Maggie and Marta Dugan were the same person. Identical twins, born four minutes apart. Marta was the older one. She was also the bossy one, which left Maggie to be compliant. That was about the only difference between them. People outside the family usually couldn't tell them apart. Their parents, brothers, and sisters knew that Maggie's nose bent ever so slightly to the left, and that Marta had a small mole on her right earlobe. Their blonde hair was the exact same shade. In both girls it was wavy. Their brown eyes were the same dark chocolate. They grew at the same rate, lost their baby teeth at the same time, caught all the same colds and flu viruses, had chicken pox in tandem, and required braces by their ninth birthday.

Now in their fourteenth year, they pulled apart. Their separation was caused by a boy. Chad Stockton had expressed a distinct preference for Maggie, and since his choice couldn't be based on physical factors, the girls were at a loss. Or rather, Marta was at a loss. Their classmates knew perfectly well that Chad liked Maggie because she was sweet and docile, and always saw the good in people. She was even a bit gullible, a trait Chad hoped would eventually work to his advantage. Marta, on the other hand, was cranky and suspicious, like her mother. There had been some experience with the mother at school-sponsored events. A bake sale, in particular, came to mind. The mother had slapped one student's hand for reaching toward a brownie she hadn't yet paid for. Another student had been called a "crude hick."

To the twins, Chad's attachment to Maggie caused the river they'd been on their whole life to change course. While Maggie made her way to shore, Marta drifted down the rapids. She dyed her hair black, and like her older sister, Angie, got a nose ring. Maggie was appalled. Lavinia threatened to tie a string through it and lead her around the way you would a bull. Chip avoided looking at it until it had healed. Timothy said she was stupid, and Foster just wanted to know how much it had hurt.

Next the twins wanted to have separate rooms. They'd always shared, and their request came as a shock. Chip's home had five bedrooms, all currently occupied since Angie was still living at home while she went to the state university over in Cortland. A small sewing room at the end of the hall had been the private retreat and sanctuary of Chip's late wife. She'd been dead for fifteen years, and the room hadn't been touched. Alma dusted it once a month, and every time she went in and opened the shutters, she thought what a nice little place it could be, if all the junk were cleared away.

Marta claimed the sewing room without consulting anyone. She went in, pushed the old chair into the hall, then the writing desk that still had paper and pens on it, then the books about embroidery and flower arranging were stacked on the floor outside the door. There were a lot of knick-knacks. The woman seemed to have had a passion for zebras. There were china figurines, glass statues, even a framed print, all of zebras. Inside the writing desk, Marta found a small, leather-bound book. She opened it. In someone's very exacting script were the words *Wayne has not behaved himself at all today.* She read some more passages at random. They seemed to be a chronicle of the Starkhurst boys when they were children. Marta had met Chip's son, Ethan, three years before, but not the other two, who lived in Texas. The author, clearly the late Mrs. Starkhurst, observed her children dispassionately, even coldly at times. She wondered if Chip knew the diary was there, or if he wanted to have it. She thought of asking Maggie her opinion, because she was used to asking Maggie her opinion on everything. Under the circumstances, she refused. It was then that she experienced, for the

94

first time in her life, a sudden, almost sickening rush of loneliness. She put the book away and left the room.

Lavinia wasn't happy with the mess at the end of the hall. Moving the chair and desk to the basement fell to Timothy and Chip. Foster was still too small at twelve to be of much use lifting furniture. Once they'd done that, Lavinia asked Marta what she intended to do about a bed. The one in the room she shared with Maggie was a double. There was no chance of it clearing the door of the sewing room. Marta didn't admit that she hadn't thought of that. She said she'd use a sleeping bag on the floor until a new single bed could be bought. Lavinia was annoyed. She pointed out that beds cost money, and that Marta hadn't considered that. Marta was unmoved. She knew how well-off they were. In the last year, Lavinia had finally quit working because Chip had wanted her to all along. Now she spent her days playing golf in the summer, or ice-skating in the winter. No one quite understood her love of skating. She said she'd skated as a girl and had always wanted to take it up again. True, she was quite graceful out there on the ice, because even after five children she'd maintained a slim figure. When she wasn't doing either of those, she was helping run one of the new art galleries down on the Dunston Commons. She knew nothing about art, but she liked to be around nice things, so Chip arranged a position for her with the wife of one of his old friends.

Lavinia gave in on the bed quickly enough. Other modest furniture was purchased at the same time, and within a matter of a few days, Marta had a place she called her own. No one was allowed in, except Alma, and Top, Marta's cat. Top's brother, Tip, stayed in Maggie's room. The cats had slept together since they were kittens and didn't bear their separation nearly as well as Maggie and Marta did. Or at least, as they appeared to. Secretly they each thought things had gone a bit too far, but Marta wouldn't relent. She hoped Maggie was happy, all alone there in her huge, empty-feeling room, where she could dream the night away about Chad Stockton.

Maggie didn't dream about Chad Stockton. Nor did she give

him any thought when she was awake. She thought he was a dork, and always had. She'd never shared Marta's enthusiasm for him. She just didn't say so. Marta had quickly assumed that the attraction was mutual. It wasn't. But since Marta was being a butt, in Maggie's opinion, she kept quiet and watched Marta send him desperate glances at school.

Eventually the cats brought things to a head. Top clawed at Marta's door all night, wanting to be let free to find Tip. Tip did the same thing to Maggie's door. The girls tried shutting them out at bedtime, but then they roamed the house and wrought havoc. They scratched the expensive new silk-upholstered furniture Lavinia had bought for the living room. They shattered an expensive vase on the dining room table. The obvious solution was to keep both cats in the same room. The girls couldn't decide who should have them, and Lavinia didn't want to lay down the law. She was trying to take a fairer approach to things. But she did tell them that they'd simply have to come up with some sort of solution, or it was possible that both cats would have to be found another home.

And so they made a pact. There'd be a competition—a dare—and the winner would get to say. This was new ground. In the past they'd always worked together. As to the dare itself, that was up to each girl to plan, then execute. No discussion would be allowed. Neither really knew how judging would take place, and thought they'd figure it out later.

Maggie was stumped. She had no idea what she could do to top Marta. Marta was already out in front with her crazy hair, nose ring, and now metal-studded pants. As she considered various options, she realized that a successful dare was one that did a lot more than raise eyebrows. She needed to make people sit up and take notice.

What if she glued someone's locker shut? Or stuck gum on her history teacher's chair? But those were pranks, stupid ones at that. The dare had been Marta's idea, and Maggie was certain that she was planning something pretty wild. And courageous, because she, like

Maggie, would quickly have seen that this dare needed to exhibit bravery, not sneaky antics.

A new boy had recently transferred to the school. He was openly gay. Most people didn't really care, but some did. There were taunts, ugly names called, his backpack thrown in the toilet. What if Maggie befriended him? Made him her special project? Then she, too, would be the object of scorn. She wasn't sure she was tough enough to last it out. Marta would be, though.

Maggie considered all of this as she rode the bus home alone. Marta now took a different bus to further the spirit of independence. Maggie missed her. It felt strange to admit that to herself. There was no one in the world she knew better than Marta, but now she didn't know her at all, it seemed.

A very fat woman with stringy hair got on at the next top. She was holding the hand of a little girl, whom she hauled up the stairs behind her. The little girl was Annabelle, from Angie's picnic the summer before. The woman must be her mother. It had been Annabelle's grandmother who brought her to the lake, and the one who'd belted her hard enough to send food out of her mouth. Annabelle now had glasses that did little to hide her tiny eyes. She walked pigeon-toed down the aisle, her elbows out for balance. The woman pointed to a seat by the window. Annabelle took it. The woman lowered herself into the aisle seat. They were two rows ahead of Maggie.

A gentle rain fell. Drops rolled down the window where Annabelle sat, and she followed one with her finger. She hummed. She swung her legs. She bounced up and down. Her mother told her to stop. Annabelle didn't stop. Her mother pinched her fat arm. Annabelle squealed, then grabbed a handful of her mother's ratty hair.

"I told you a hundred times, don't do that!" her mother said. Annabelle resumed her humming.

Two boys with earphones boarded the bus. The clomped down the aisle. One looked at Annabelle and laughed. He pulled his friend's sleeve, and the friend looked, too. The friend made a face at Annabelle.

Annabelle didn't see. She was tracking raindrops again. Annabelle's mother saw.

"Hey, fuckface! Why don't you get your faggot ass out of here?" she said. The boys might not have heard her words, because of the earphones, but they saw her expression. They moved off quickly.

Maggie remembered Annabelle at the picnic. She'd held Angie's hand almost the whole time. That meant she was sweet natured and loving. Those things made up for what she lacked in brains. Being stupid wasn't her fault. One look at the mother and you knew where the fault lay. She probably did something she shouldn't have when she was pregnant. She obviously didn't take very good care of herself. She was two hundred pounds, at least.

They came to the last stop in downtown before the bus made its way along the lakeshore. Annabelle's mother stood up and jerked Annabelle's arm. Annabelle got up, too, and followed along to the front of the bus. Maggie got out of her seat and went after them. Annabelle's gait was so jerky that her Barbie backpack slapped and swayed as she went. After about half a block they entered the back door of a restaurant. It was Joe's, a low-ball Italian place Maggie used to go to when her parents were still married. She crossed the street and approached the door they'd gone in. It had a dirty, diamond-shaped window that she had to stand on tiptoe to see through. The mother was tying a white apron around her huge jiggly gut. Annabelle wasn't there. Maggie realized she was looking into a storeroom. A long stainless steel counter was visible through another doorway. That must be the kitchen. Annabelle's mother was probably one of the cooks. *Ick,* Maggie thought. *Who'd want to eat anything that pig made?* Maggie moved back, and stepped onto a piece of chewing gum. It stuck hard to the bottom of her canvas shoe. She pulled her foot up behind her, balancing awkwardly on the other, to take a look. The gum was bright purple.

Maggie looked through the window again, and saw that the mother had gone somewhere else. She opened the door and slipped quickly inside. She hoped to hell no one would see her before she found

Annabelle. But Annabelle was right there, off to one side, sitting on a cardboard box, watching a tiny black-and-white television set that was propped on a chair. Her coat was still on, and she was drinking something from a red plastic cup.

"Hi," Annabelle said. Maggie froze. Her heart was pounding. There was noise coming from the kitchen, pots banging and water running, and a loud, female voice shouting, "That'll be the day!" The voice belonged to Annabelle's mother.

"What are you doing here?" Maggie asked.

"Waiting."

"For what?"

"My mom."

"Your mom works here."

Annabelle nodded.

"When does she get done for the day?"

Annabelle shrugged. Maggie felt stupid for thinking Annabelle would know how to tell time.

"It's dark out," Annabelle said.

"No it isn't, look." Then Maggie realized that Annabelle was trying to say her mother's shift ended after it was dark. That didn't mean much. It could be a couple of hours, it could be seven or eight. And the whole time Annabelle was supposed to sit here and watch that crappy television and drink her drink. She should have company, something to eat, a place to play and run around.

Maggie took Annabelle by the hand, picked up her backpack, and led her out the door. She hustled them across the parking lot and around the corner where they couldn't be seen. Annabelle was huffing as Maggie tugged her along. Maggie's head hurt. She felt like a hero, a flashy, high-spirited angel from a better world, but she also felt like an idiot, and worse than that, she felt like a thief.

Annabelle said nothing. Maybe she thought they were playing a game.

"Hide-and-seek," Maggie said.

"Okay."

They were pressed into a tall hedge, drawing a few odd looks from people walking past them.

"Oh, man," Maggie said. It was all sinking in now, the trouble she might get in. Maybe she should just take Annabelle back and go on home alone. Annabelle pushed up the sleeve of her coat and scratched her arm. Her wrist was bruised. So was the other one.

"Come on," Maggie said. They went to the next bus stop. The gum on Maggie's shoe stuck as fiercely as before. Annabelle hummed.

"I'm hungry," she said.

"Soon."

Maggie had just been given the privilege of having her own cell phone, and she wondered now if she should call home. And say what? And to whom? Then the bus came, and she had to focus her attention on getting Annabelle on board, seated, and quiet.

By the time they reached the house, Maggie was exhausted. Annabelle was a handful! She never managed to sit still longer than a minute and kept trying to get up and out of her seat. Maggie thought she was probably confused by what was going on and didn't understand why she'd been plucked from her routine. Yet she didn't seem unhappy at all. She smiled a lot. As far as Maggie could tell, Annabelle thought they were still playing hide-and-seek.

Timothy was roller-skating in the front hall, which meant Alma had gone out. He came to a stop just in front of Annabelle.

"Hi," he said.

"Hi."

"You're the girl from the picnic."

"Picnic."

"What are you doing here?"

"She's visiting," Maggie said. "Who else is home?"

Timothy went on staring down at Annabelle. His skates gave him a four-inch advantage.

"Mom, I think. No, wait, she went to get her hair done. Chip's at the Rotary Club, unless he already came back. Foster's at soccer. Marta's somewhere. And Angie said she'd be late. Something to do with a project for one of her classes."

Maggie took Annabelle upstairs to her room. They took off their coats. Annabelle sat down on the floor. Her denim coveralls were filthy, Maggie now saw. So was her pink turtleneck. Maggie went into her closet and found a box way in the back. It was full of plastic dolls she used to play with. She'd been unable to give them up during one her mother's sudden cleaning frenzies. She put the box in front of Annabelle.

"Here. You sit here for a minute and play by yourself, okay?" she said.

"Okay."

Maggie sped down the hall to Marta's sewing closet. She banged on the door.

"Not home," Marta shouted.

Maggie opened the door.

"What the fuck do you want?" Marta asked. She was applying black polish to her toes.

"I did it."

"What?"

"The dare."

"What dare?"

"You know! The dare!"

Marta put the cap on the polish and got to her feet. The combat boots she'd worn to school were on the silk bedspread.

"Come with me," Maggie said.

"Where?"

"Hurry."

Maggie rushed down the hall. Marta hobbled along behind her. She'd stuffed cotton balls in between her toes. Annabelle wasn't in Maggie's room.

"Oh, shit!" Maggie said. She ran downstairs. Timothy had resumed his skating practice. His body was fluid and fast as he rounded the dining room table.

"She's in the kitchen," he called out over his shoulder.

Annabelle had found a box of cookies and was eating them one by one. Crumbs were down her front, and on the floor, too.

"What the hell?" Marta asked, when she got there a moment later.

"I rescued her."

Annabelle looked supremely content. "Milk," she said.

Maggie poured her a glass of milk. She used an old plastic cup decorated with yellow dinosaurs.

"You *kidnapped* her, you mean," Marta said.

"No, I didn't. She wanted to come with me, didn't you Annabelle?"

Annabelle nodded. Maggie took the chair next to her. She patted her shoulder.

"More," Annabelle said. Maggie got up and poured her a second cup of milk.

"I don't get it. Why did you bring her here?" Marta asked.

"I just said. Rescuing her was my dare. Now, what's yours?"

"What the fuck are you talking about?"

"The *dare*. The dare we made. To see who gets to have both cats in their room."

"Oh, that. Who cares? You can have 'em. Top's a pain in the ass. He keeps trying to sleep on my pillow."

"You mean, you're not going to do a dare?"

"Of course not. What do you take me for, an idiot?"

"But it was your idea!"

"Oh, so what? I didn't think you'd take me seriously."

Maggie sat down. She hadn't counted on this, that her bravery would go unmatched.

Annabelle released a long, loud fart, then giggled.

"Kid's all charm," said Marta. Timothy rolled in.

"Mom's home."

"Uh, oh."

Maggie's face was still, her lips tight.

Lavinia came into the kitchen. Her hair was frosted and feathery. Her children all thought the same thing—that she looked like a fancy chicken. She soon looked like a fancy, pissed-off chicken when the color rose in her thin face, as Maggie was forced to relay the events of that afternoon.

Lavinia went into Chip's study and poured herself a large drink. When she returned to the kitchen, Annabelle had moved on to cherry pie left over from last night's dinner. Lavinia considered her options. They weren't good. Chip would be back any minute and wouldn't be at all happy. He wouldn't say so, of course. Chip never said so. He just looked grim and disappeared for a few hours to play solitaire. Sometimes Lavinia wondered if he regretted marrying her as much as she regretted marrying him.

She returned to the kitchen and sat across from Annabelle.

"Well, we'll just have to take her back," Lavinia said.

"Wanna stay here," Annabelle said.

"You can't, dear. This isn't your home."

Annabelle's face pinched up. She rocked back and forth on her stool.

"See? You upset her," Maggie said. She patted Annabelle again.

"What if they're looking for her? What if they called the police?" Timothy asked.

Having the police show up would pretty much put her in the shithouse with Chip for quite a while, Lavinia thought.

"Well, I can call her grandmother, I suppose," Lavinia said. "At least tell her that she's here."

"What about her mom?" Marta asked.

Lavinia hadn't thought about that.

"Dear, whom should I call? Your mother, or your grandmother?" Lavinia asked Annabelle.

"Granny. Granny likes me."

Everyone remembered Cici Sloan hitting Annabelle.

"All right, dear. That's a good idea."

The Sloans weren't listed. Lavinia said that figured. They were probably avoiding bill collectors. They looked through Annabelle's backpack. A phone number was written on the inside in magic marker. It turned out to be Cici's. Lavinia explained that Annabelle had come home with Maggie. That's all she would say. Cici didn't ask any questions. She just said she'd be along in a bit. Neither she nor Lavinia mentioned notifying Annabelle's mother.

After getting off the phone, Lavinia helped herself to another drink. Chip came home from his meeting. He was cheerful. The Rotary Club was in the process of awarding its annual scholarships to worthy high school seniors. One of the recipients was a boy who reminded Chip very much of himself at that age, without the funding Chip had had, of course. The boy was tall and lean, well-spoken, and completely earnest. At least, that's how Chip preferred to remember himself.

Lavinia told him they had a visitor. She explained.

"The little girl from the picnic? Oh, well, that's great! She seemed like such a nice little thing," he said. It was his turn to help himself to the liquor cabinet.

The twins, Timothy, and Annabelle had all returned to Maggie's room. Timothy was reading, stretched out on Maggie's bed. He still had his skates on. Marta was putting black eyeliner on Annabelle, who enjoyed it so far. Maggie was still glum. She felt like the butt of a very mean joke, almost as if someone had rigged a bucket of water to fall on her head, or had taped a silly note on her back that said *Kick Me.*

Downstairs, Cici had arrived. She'd lost weight, and her hair was different. Tinted, Lavinia thought. She wondered if she were still seeing Potter. She liked to think Potter wouldn't spend time with a woman who smacked children around. Lavinia invited Cici to sit down. She even offered her a drink, which to her surprise Cici refused.

"I remember riding my bike past this barn back in the day," Cici said. "Funny to think someone I know lives here now."

"Annabelle's upstairs."

"She give you any trouble?"

"No."

"That's a first. She can be pretty frisky."

Lavinia wondered about the bruises on Annabelle's wrists that Maggie had pointed out.

"She's worst at school. I mean, all the other kids are—delayed somehow, but she's the pushiest," Cici said.

"She doesn't seem that way."

"Not when she's in a new place. But, once she gets her feet under her, watch out."

"Don't you need to call her mother?"

"Nah. Annabelle does this a lot."

"Does what?"

"Ups and leaves. She takes herself on the bus all over Dunston. She makes her way back before too long."

"You're kidding!"

"Hey, she's slow, but she's not a complete moron."

Lavinia thought about this. Maybe Annabelle pretended to be dumber than she was. She'd probably learned that it had its perks.

Lavinia offered Cici a cup of coffee.

"Can I change my mind about that drink?" Cici asked.

"Of course."

Lavinia brought out a nice bottle of Chablis, though she figured Cici probably wouldn't know the difference.

As she drank, Cici became pleasant, not at all the way she was at the picnic. She mentioned a man named Ed a number of times in connection with some household matter, like repairing a door, or rebuilding the motor on her clothes dryer.

"I'm sorry, who's Ed again?" Lavinia asked.

"Oh. Never said, did I? Ed's my husband."

"Husband."

"Second husband. As of about three months ago."

So much for her taking up with Potter, Lavinia thought.

"What's he do?" Lavinia asked.

"Drives a bus. That's how come I know about Annabelle. She gets on his route sometimes. He sort of keeps an eye out for her. The other drivers all know her, too. They call in if she shows up on one of theirs."

"That's nice."

Cici shrugged. "She's a handful, like I say. Was harder than hell on Norma—my daughter—when we realized what we were dealing with. I even thought about sending her away, you know to an institution, but Norma wouldn't have it. I feel bad, when I think about it sometimes."

"It's only natural to want to get out from under a problem."

"God's truth. Only kids are one problem you never really get out from under, are they?"

They talked about people they'd known in school. Baxter Bain now sold real estate. His signs were all over the place. And Lisa Toterhouse ran a hair salon on the Commons. Cici knew more about what their classmates had gone on to do than Lavinia did. She'd never cared or bothered to look back. For her, it had been full steam ahead. Marriage, children, building a career because she had to.

"I knew her. His late wife," Cici said.

"Whose wife? Chip's?"

"She used to come into my uncle's hardware store. Always wanted something to feed her roses with. Or fencing to put around them to keep the deer away."

There weren't any rose bushes on the property. Maybe Chip had torn them out when she died. He'd been pretty busted up over it, though he never used those words to Lavinia. *Rather knocked the wind out of me,* was how he put it.

From upstairs came an angry howl. Then Timothy came clumsily down the stairs, clutching the rail, so his skates wouldn't go out from under him. He rolled slowly into the living room and stopped at the edge of the oriental rug.

"She hit me. I was reading, and she wanted to see the book, and I said I'd show her in a minute, and she hit me!"

"Annabelle?"

"Who else?"

"See what I mean? Doesn't get her way, and BAM," Cici said.

There were more voices, and the sound of a door closing.

"I better get her out of here before she brings the place down around your ears," Cici said.

The twins escorted Annabelle downstairs. Marta looked cross, and Maggie looked embarrassed.

"She's not having fun anymore," Marta said.

Annabelle looked down, then right at her grandmother. Her eyeliner was all smudged.

"You tell this nice boy you're sorry for beaning him, you hear?" Cici said.

"Sorry."

"That's better."

"At school they just hit her back. This one girl dragged her all over the playroom, she got so ticked. Annabelle's no lightweight, either. Must have been a sight," Cici said.

Later, after dinner, Marta came into Maggie's room. She had Top with her. The cat wriggled free. He walked around the room, peering into corners, then trotted out the door. Maggie didn't want him, or Tip either, for that matter, and told Marta so.

"I hate those stupid cats."

"They're just cats. Timothy said he'd take them," said Marta.

Maggie wished he'd volunteered to before all of this had happened.

"You really were never going to do a dare?" she asked.

"Nuh-uh."

And Maggie probably wouldn't have, either, if she hadn't seen Annabelle get on the bus with her mother. Even though she didn't get in trouble, she felt like an idiot for coming to the rescue of someone who didn't need her to. It hadn't made any difference that everyone

OUR LOVE COULD LIGHT THE WORLD

said her heart was in the right place. She'd been duped, and by her own twin sister.

"I'm thinking of moving back in here," Marta said.

"Why?"

"I don't know. That other room's too small. And I miss the fireplace."

The fireplace was the best feature of the room. She and Maggie used to sit by it all winter long and talk about things neither of them could remember at the moment.

Maggie had gotten used to having the place to herself. She put away the toys Annabelle had played with and smoothed out the bedspread where Timothy had lain with his skates. She organized the make-up Marta had used on Annabelle and handed it back to her.

"I can't wait to tell Chad all about this tomorrow. He won't believe it," Maggie said. Hurt and anger flashed in Marta's eyes. She snatched her make-up case out of Maggie's hand and left. A few seconds later, Maggie heard the door of the sewing room slam shut.

Maggie didn't feel good about what she'd said. She didn't like upsetting people. But in Marta's case, after all the trouble she'd caused, it was only fair.

THE CONCEPT OF KINDNESS

Angie found that the best time to compose emails was late at night, when no one else in the house was awake, except the cats, Tip and Top, who wandered in and occasionally jumped onto her computer keyboard.

Dear Aunt Patty:

School is going fine. I like my classes pretty well. I'm thinking about majoring in social work. I figure there are a lot of losers out there who wouldn't be losers if someone had given them a chance.

Here she paused and thought about her father, Potter. She wondered if Patty thought of him that way, too.

Not sure exactly how you turn a loser into a non-loser (or should I say winner?) but I figure it's worth looking into. Talk soon. Angie.

Patty seemed to be the one person she could share her thoughts with these days, maybe because she was at a safe distance out in Montana, which as the crow flies was a good eighteen hundred miles. Sometimes Angie thought about those miles she'd driven with her father, and saw by bus alone on the return trip. The land did funny things along the way. First it was hilly and green the way it was all around Dunston. Then it flattened out, but was still mostly green. Then the trees disappeared and the land was even flatter, with gold and brown grasses. Western Montana got hilly once more, and then there were snow-capped peaks on the horizon. The light made all the shadows hard and sharp, and the wind seemed to blow all the time.

Angie always wrote about life in general, never anything specific. The only specific thing she'd mention would be that she was in love with Blake Rawls, a professor of psychology who served as an adjunct to the School of Social Work. Everything about him made Angie ache. His ponytail, his biceps, and the diamond earring in his left earlobe had taken firm root in her heart and pulled her along. And so she went. All one hundred and sixty pounds of her. But at nineteen, she wasn't ugly. She had a fine face. A small nose and soft, wide-set eyes made a prettiness. Even the mirror in the women's room of Andrews Hall, splotched with black, told her so. She went there when it got to be too much. His piercing blue eyes. The drops of sweat that formed on his brow when he talked about the state of social work today. Assessing the dysfunctional family. Learning how to be invisible enough to get through the door, and then finding the strength to be impassive, yet fully aware of what's at stake. *Ears and eyes, people. Then invoking the force of the law, that's always your side. The trick is to get them to trust you, feel completely at ease. Then when you take their kids away, there's less drama. Always give them hope that their parental rights can be reinstated. Otherwise they often become hopeless, even more destructive than they were.*

He stood there, arms crossed, as if that concept of kindness was hard-learned. As if it had cost him.

For the winter quarter, Angie had the chance to apply for an internship. To learn firsthand what it was like to call on people in distressed situations. Professor Rawls was taking a break from teaching then. He was writing a book and needed to gather fresh material. All the women students applied. Angie's application was selected. She was speechless. She was summoned. She brought a plate of cookies.

His office had a large window that looked down on the main quad. On the bookshelves were titles like *Man's Inhumanity To Man, The Ancient Greeks, Medieval Thought and Philosophy, Baroque Architecture.* His swivel chair creaked when it spun. The desk had a roll-top. There were photographs of beaches, palm trees, a woman with long black hair on the walls. She was too pretty, and too thin. Angie didn't like that Professor Rawls had been to the tropics, had lain on white sand by blue water, his mind far from home.

He invited her to sit. There was a metal folding chair that had her several inches lower than he was. He apologized for that. His Harvard chair was out for repairs, he said.

"Harvard chair?"

"For surviving their doctoral program."

"Oh."

"You know where Harvard is, don't you?"

"Boston."

"Cambridge."

"I thought that was in England."

Professor Rawls smiled. "You'll make a first-rate social worker," he said.

"Really? Why?"

"You're honest about your mistakes."

Heat rose in Angie's cheeks. It wasn't a mistake to say that Cambridge was in England when it was. How the hell was she supposed to know that there was another one?

"Don't be upset. Mistakes are learning moments," he said.

He outlined the details of her internship. She would earn five credits, the same as if she'd taken a class. She'd work with the Department of Social Services in the field, interview people, and write reports. These would be observations, recommendations. She was to bring fresh eyes to every problem and keep an open mind. It all sounded both terrifying and exciting.

"Any questions?" Professor Rawls asked. He leaned back in his squeaky chair and gave her a long, cool stare. He hadn't shaved, Angie noticed. His stubble had white in it. He didn't look old enough for that. His hair had no gray, only copper highlights among the ash-blond. He was fond of turquoise jewelry. He wore a large blue stone, flecked with gold and green, on an ornate silver band. It was on his wedding finger.

His belt buckle was silver and turquoise, also. On the wall behind his desk was on odd circular form, webbed, with feathers hanging from it. He saw where she was looking.

"That's a Navajo dream-catcher. Supposed to filter out your bad dreams, and let you have only good ones," he said.

"Does it work?"

He laughed. "Can't really say. I'd have to bring it home, put it over my bed. Don't do too much sleeping here in the office."

"Why did you choose me?"

His hands clasped behind his head. The underarms of his denim shirt were dark with sweat. She wondered if he were nervous.

"For the internship? Because you're the best."

Angie wanted to believe him. She really did. She committed herself to try.

Misery has a smell all its own, Aunt Patty. You can't believe how some people live. I mean there's dirt, and then there's filth. What Angie didn't say was that some places reminded her a lot of the ones she'd lived in with her family before her mother left and married Chip Starkhurst. The last one in particular hit a little close to home. She'd gone there with Bonita, a social worker for the County. Professor Rawls—Blake, as Angie now called him—thought they'd be a good match. Bonita was in her forties, cynical, abrupt, and unsympathetic. Oh, Angie knew all about how social workers burned out after a while, when the real struggle became how to keep yourself committed and effective. They'd done a whole segment on that in class. She was sure that Blake wanted her to taste the real life she was aiming for, and be guided by a true veteran.

Bonita took her to a place out in the country. There'd been complaints that the children weren't attending school on a regular basis. The children—four in all—ranged in age from five to twelve. They lived with their mother. No one knew where the father was. The mother had more than forty cats and dogs. A large room in the back of the house was given over to crates and food bowls. The cats slept on the stove and the kitchen counters. Angie even found two curled up in a bathtub that was ringed with gray. The dogs were outside in a big run. Some had mange. Others had goopy discharge in their eyes.

It wasn't the animals that bothered Angie, but the grim efforts of the children to keep order in their environment. They skipped school to feed the animals, cook, and take care of their mother who seemed capable of nothing but lying on the couch with a wet washcloth on her forehead. In Angie's own personal experience it was Lavinia—her mother—who'd saved them from social workers by doing everything she and Angie's father were supposed to do together. Angie realized that one person could accomplish a great deal, and that sometimes only one person was needed to stand between you and the world.

"When we get back to the office, call the SPCA. Tell them to get over there and see if they take custody of the animals," Bonita said.

"But why?"

"What do mean, why? The place stinks of dog shit. The cats are thin as rails. That fool woman doesn't have enough money to feed her own kids, let alone all these damn animals."

Where was that concept of kindness now? Angie wondered.

Bonita drove slowly, like an old woman. She glanced at Angie.

"How do you like Blake?" Bonita asked.

"He's okay."

The flush in Angie's cheeks soon proved what a huge understatement she'd made.

"You know, in the ten years I've known him, he's never had a male intern."

"Really?"

"Really."

Angie didn't like the sound of that.

"He's what my mother would call a real, old-fashioned wolf."

"No, he's not."

"He make a pass at you, yet?"

"Of course not!"

"Only a matter of time. Mark my words. And when he does, you stand your ground if you know what's good for you."

Angie turned away and stared crossly out the window.

"Let's just say I've been down a few roads you'd be smart not to travel," Bonita said.

I can't make out what she meant by that, Aunt Patty. Did she mean that she and Professor Rawls had a relationship? What do you think?

I think you're right, Ange. Sounds like he can't keep it in his pants. I say keep your guard up. A word to the wise. Love, Patty.

But it too was late for that. Blake invited her to his home for lunch one Saturday, and they spent the afternoon in bed. At first, Angie was thrilled. She was twenty years old, and it was high time she lost her virginity. Other than that, nothing was as she expected. He offered her a drink, even though she was underage, and she took it. He didn't bother with small talk. He said he wanted to have sex with her, and he assumed she was all right with that. The business-like approach was confusing, and she told him so. He said it had been his experience that young women had romantic ideas that were best put to rest at the outset.

So there won't be any misunderstanding, or false hopes. That's just how he put it, Aunt Patty. I'm very impressed with his honesty.

That was a lie. His "honesty" made her feel ordinary, like all the ones who'd come before. He admitted to nothing, because she didn't ask.

Then it became a routine. Wednesdays and Saturdays, always at his place. She lay in his bed and stared at the artwork on the walls. The abstract prints didn't calm her anxiety. All those swirling red masses, like injured hearts, looking down at her while Blake showered. He always showered afterwards.

Like he can't wait to wash me off, Aunt Patty. What does that mean?

That e-mail, and the one before it went unanswered, because she never sent them. She'd grown embarrassed at her candor, and had to think that Patty, had she read them, would tell her to stop being a fool. *Take yourself in hand, and get the hell out of there!* And she'd be right.

Sex, Angie discovered, only deepened her hunger for Blake. She couldn't fathom his casual approach to it all. She reminded herself how many women he'd had, whereas he was the only man she'd been to bed with. Sometimes, in the heat of it, he became someone else, urgent and tender. Then, on his feet and back in his clothes, he was aloof while she tried to gain his attention. She kept hoping that he'd be the same out of bed as he was in. He wasn't. It drove her crazy.

Haven't heard from you in a while. Hope everything's okay, and that you're steering clear of that creepy professor. When older men go for younger women, it means they're on a power trip. Trust me on that one.

Oddly enough, Patty's words gave Angie a little measure of courage. Patty was no fool. Angie was the fool. She didn't like feeling that way, and she slumped.

"You look like you've been through the shredder," Bonita said. Her office was small, hot, and smelled of disinfectant. She'd trimmed her afro, and her head seemed huge.

"I'm fine."

"Good. You ready to go see the Grangers?"

"Little girl keeps showing up with bruises?"

"That's the one. Today's the day we take her out and get her in foster care."

"Jesus."

"Don't think he's got much to do with it."

And then the first thing Angie noticed was the cross around Mrs. Granger's neck. Her face was young, and her hands were old, gnarled, as if they'd been broken and put back together the wrong way. Mrs. Granger saw Angie looking at them.

"Arthritis. Rheumatoid. Had it since I was a kid," Mrs. Granger said. She had a walker behind the chair she was sitting in.

Bonita was at the table, too, going over the conditions that must be met for her daughter's return. She was to have no unsupervised contact with the father, which meant the father would have to move out in order for the daughter to live at home.

"Making me choose," Mrs. Granger said. "Isn't that a hell of a thing?"

On the drive over, Bonita told Angie that Mrs. Granger had, in essence, stood by while the husband hit the child. Angie didn't see how Bonita knew that for sure. The little girl had been extensively interviewed. She said her mother was always home when her father got mad at her. Looking at Mrs. Granger now, Angie couldn't imagine her coming to anyone's aid. The woman could barely walk, had trouble standing, and was in obvious pain. It didn't seem right that she should lose her child, even temporarily, because someone had been stronger and crueler than she was.

Mrs. Granger was a pretty woman, Angie decided. Small, delicate features showed well with her hair up the way it was. The house was spotless. Surfaces were clear. Sofa cushions all in place. The idea that Mrs. Granger had struggled, in her condition, to put everything right probably in order to show that her home was the best place for the child made Angie feel sick.

The girl emerged from a back room. She looked a little like Mrs. Granger, with the same small nose and pointed chin. She had a black eye and a cut on one cheek. That, too, made Angie feel sick. The child had a small pink and white suitcase with her. She hung back until Mrs. Granger summoned her forward.

"This is Beth," Mrs. Granger said.

"I'm Angie."

Beth stared up at Angie and blinked. Angie couldn't tell how old she was. Maybe four or five.

"You're going to come with us for a little while. Just for a little while,"

Angie said. She looked up to find Bonita giving her a hard stare. Bonita left a folder on the table with Mrs. Granger. She held out her hand. Beth didn't move. Mrs. Granger nudged her gently in Bonita's direction.

"Well, looks like you've done a good job and gotten yourself ready," Bonita said. "Your mother is very proud of you."

"I don't want to go," Beth said.

"I know. But you'll see, you'll have a lot of fun in your new home."

"I want to stay here."

"Beth," Mrs. Granger said. "None of that. I told you."

Beth's face went slack. Her eyes were dull. She hugged her mother, then picked up her suitcase and walked towards the door. Angie went after her.

"Call me in about a week. Give me a progress report on your husband. We'll see about you and Beth having a visit then," Bonita told Mrs. Granger.

"Sure." Mrs. Granger sounded like she didn't believe a word of it.

With Beth in the back seat, they drove to the office, where her foster parents were waiting to take her home. Angie excused herself from that part. Bonita had no choice but to make a note of Angie's abrupt departure in her file.

Blake asked to see her. He wanted to go over her lackluster reports. His exact words. He took her out for coffee. She assumed they'd be going to his place. She asked why they hadn't. He said it was best to be in a neutral atmosphere. Angie swallowed hard. She asked if he were breaking up with her. He said they'd never really been together. Angie's hands went cold, then numb. She was weeping before she knew it. He handed her a napkin and told her to pull herself together. He said he'd walk out if she didn't stop. He stood to go, and she grabbed his arm. In the process she sent her cup of coffee to the floor. He asked her to look at what she'd done. The server came to clean it up. Blake stayed only a few moments longer, then left. When Angie finally got to her feet, and made her way into the twilight she hadn't expected to see, having lost track of time, she realized he hadn't mentioned her reports at all. His asking to see her had had nothing to do with the internship. All he'd wanted was to get rid of her.

Finally Lavinia had to pin her down and make her say what was wrong. She'd never seen Angie that way. She told Chip it was completely unlike her to take to her bed over anything. To find out that it was about a man made sense. She'd guessed as much. She hadn't thought the man was a professor. She needed to know more, so Chip did some checking. He had contacts at the university. He phoned the vice president, yet another golf buddy. Professor Rawls had been through a devastating divorce years before. Since then he'd been involved with a number of young women students over the years. None had ever made an official complaint against him, however. There had never been a case of sexual harassment filed. It was unseemly for a man in his position to date his students, the vice president said, but everyone knew it happened. Rawls had been successful in getting federal funding for a number of research projects, and given that his field was psychology, never very high on anyone's list of priorities, the university had been willing to look the other way in the matter of his personal affairs. Chip shared this information with Lavinia. Neither talked about it with Angie.

She missed two weeks of school, and there was some concern that she'd have to repeat the quarter. Chip made another call, and explained that she was ill. She was granted another week. Her brothers and sisters walked quietly past her closed door. Sometimes they brought her a bowl of chicken soup, leftover Chinese food, or her favorite, cold pizza with a topping of onion and black olives. They all knew what had happened without being told. They were sensitive that way.

Their kindness touched her. Soon it was worth more than Blake's embrace. Maybe she wasn't a loser, after all. Maybe she was just like everyone else. She went back to class. She didn't have to see Blake. She submitted her observations to him via email. His replies were simple.

Thanks and *Good job.* She tried not to read between the lines because she knew there was nothing deeper to find. She went to Bonita's office twice a week to sort through paperwork and review files. Bonita hadn't taken her on any more fieldwork. Angie had to think it was because she'd reacted badly with the Grangers.

Weeks passed. As Angie became calmer and less anguished, Lavinia got madder and madder at Professor Rawls. Angie had been vulnerable because she'd been inexperienced, and while it was fine to say that a hard knock was the best teacher, Lavinia thought it was criminal. He'd preyed on her daughter. Taken an obvious advantage. All her life she'd hated people like that. Someone, long ago, had once done that to her. Just an ordinary person, someone close in age, a boy who was training one summer to be a farrier. He came to the stable on campus where Lavinia's father worked, and she fell in love. That was the simple part. The hard part was disentangling herself from what became a very one-sided relationship. The boy plied her with compliments and small gifts to get her in bed. Afterwards his kind attentions stopped. When she asked why, he said there was no point spending money on her when he'd already scored. Those were his very words. Remembering that now was still painful.

She contacted Professor Rawls and told him she was interested in hiring him for a special project that would help the underprivileged of Dunston. As a professor, she felt sure he'd be able to offer valuable input into ways to improve the state's social service network. He'd work in a consulting capacity, an advisory role. He played hard to get. He said his schedule was awfully full, what with teaching. Lavinia was tempted to let slip that she knew he was on leave and didn't. She thought it best to go along.

They were to meet at Madeleine's for lunch. Lavinia applied glitter to her eyelids. Then she chose her best suit, a lavender silk jacket and skirt. She bought it at a vintage store in Wilkes-Barre years before, when she went to a conference. She didn't tell Chip what she was doing, because he'd probably object.

She asked for a table in the back, cozily set by a partition, where they could speak privately. She lit a cigarette without asking Rawls if he minded. She liked smoking sometimes, she said, though her husband didn't approve. It was his understanding that she'd quit. She supposed it wasn't completely honest to deceive him like that, but what the hell? She had to live a little sometimes, right?

She could see in his eyes that he found her attractive. Very attractive, actually. Her pulse was rapid. She didn't think she could go through with it, but then she thought of Angie, curled up in her bed crying.

He ordered a whiskey, neat. She asked for a glass of sherry.

"You know, I can't help thinking you once had a student who was an old, dear friend of mine," Lavinia said.

"Really? Who's that?"

"Claire Maltby."

"Hm. Doesn't ring a bell. But then, I've had a lot of young people come through my lecture hall."

"Yes."

Lavinia didn't have a friend named Claire Maltby. Claire Maltby was the name on the label inside her 1960s lavender suit.

"Most of them women, I'd imagine. It seems as if social work draws so many more women than men, wouldn't you say?" Lavinia asked.

"That used to be the case. But as with other fields, say for instance nursing—" and here he had a large swallow of his drink— "more men are coming up the ranks."

"Isn't that interesting? But if you ask me, I'd much rather have a female nurse, wouldn't you? I mean, it just seems more natural."

Get on with it, she told herself. *You're babbling!*

She could see him waiting for her to speak. He looked eager, greedy. The thought of that money he'd have to spend, the trips he'd justify as research-based, the young interns he'd travel with.

His turquoise ring was too large for his short, fat finger. He had the hands of a gardener, maybe, or a baker, not a professor. Those hands had been all over Angie. Lavinia put down her drink. It wasn't sitting all that well.

"Young women can be so determined, don't you think? I mean, in my day, not that I'm old, really—" she forced a silly giggle— "women were sometimes so soft. Pliable. Not made of really firm stuff, if you know what I mean."

It was obvious that he had no idea what she talking about. He finished his drink.

"Now, take my friend Claire, for instance. She got involved with someone. A professor, actually. We all thought it was wrong, that she was in way over her head, but she just couldn't seem to help herself. He had some . . . hold over her. Some power. Of course, she was an easy mark. Didn't have much in the way of self-esteem. Bit overweight, not the brightest or highest achieving person. But she had a good heart."

Professor Rawls leaned back in his chair. A moment before he'd been forward, elbows on the table. His face was damp. He looked around for the waiter, who wasn't there. Watching him, Lavinia's heart slowed. Her cheeks took on a pleasant glow.

"Of course, she was much more attached to him than he was to her. Seems as if he made a habit of sleeping with students. His, anyone's, really. Guess that made him democratic." Again the silly little giggle. "But she took it hard when he let her go. Shoved her out, was more like it. She went all to pieces, poor Claire. We all rallied around her. Tried to prop her up. It was no good. No good at all. She killed herself that winter. Hanged herself in her father's barn."

The waiter asked if they cared for another drink. Rawls said no. Lavinia said yes.

"Never like talking business on an empty stomach. I learned that from my husband. You've heard of him? Chip Starkhurst?" Lavinia asked.

"Big local real estate family, I think."

"Exactly."

Lavinia thought she was awfully clever. Angie went by Dugan. He wasn't connecting them at all.

"Very big on charitable donations," she said. That wasn't true. The Rotary Club was the only thing Chip ever gave money too. That and his three sons. Ethan had asked for help with a down payment on a house in Paolo Alto. The boys in Texas, Wayne and Chip Jr., were in business together and had had a bad year because of the recession.

"Which is why I contacted you. I'd like to do something in memory of Claire. A special curriculum that deals with mental illness in young women, maybe, or trains social workers to be specially alert to the dangers of predatory men. I'm a bit fuzzy on the details. I'll rely on you to flesh it out."

Lavinia looked at her watch. She was running late, she said. She was awfully sorry to cut short their appointment. She shook his hand, which was as damp as his face. Then she was gone without paying for their drinks. She figured that was up to him. As she drove back towards Dunston, enjoying the effects of the sherry and her words on Professor Rawls—he'd gone pale at the end, there—she thought it was possible that he'd try to contact her. Though she hadn't left him a phone number, he could always look her up. Then she thought it unlikely. She'd scared him, and he looked like the kind of man who'd turn tail and run.

Dear Aunt Patty. My spring quarter is going much better now that I finished my internship. Being back in class isn't as boring as I thought it would be. I have all new professors. Sometimes I think of the people I met out in the field, and wonder how they're getting along. My supervisor, Bonita, said I was too attached and had to learn some distance. I suppose that's a good lesson for life, in general. That's about it for now. Except that the professor I had last fall, the one I wrote you about, took a new job out-of-state. Seems weird that he'd leave after being here so long. Oh, well. You know what they say about greener

pastures. Also, Mom's been strange. She's super pleased with herself, like she's got a big fat secret she's dying to tell. Chip keeps asking her if she's got good news, meaning is she pregnant again, and she tells him to shut it. So, as you can see, here at the Dugan-Starkhurst mansion, all is well.

THE SORROW OF
THE COUNTRY

When Potter grew restless, which he did every year about this time as the hills greened and the sky lifted, he took to the road. Not as some did. Not like a long distance traveler, and not at all like Patty who, all those years before, simply couldn't take the sorrow of the country anymore and lit on out to Montana. Where they called their country Big Sky. Potter had been there once, and he'd admired its grandeur. The sweeping vistas. The stars so bright they called out your name.

But to his mind and heart there was no country like the rolling hills of upstate New York. The roads he drove followed creeks that rushed with snowmelt, past fields that should be cleared and sewn. The beauty of the land wasn't marred by the hard times visible in the fences that leaned or fell down, the barns with missing roofs, the houses that hadn't been painted in over twenty years. People were moving away, except in the town of Dunston where the university kept a steady population employed. Potter himself had had a hard winter. In the fall he'd worked on the campus grounds crew. With the cold he was laid off. He wasn't sure he'd be taken on again. There'd been a disagreement with his supervisor over putting in for unauthorized overtime. Potter didn't get the extra payment, and so didn't see what the problem was. The supervisor said it spoke volumes about a man's character that he would game the system. Potter wasn't trying to game the system. He just hadn't understood the protocol. After that he'd cut back his drinking to weekends only. Being sober five days a week had left his mind in a state of painful clarity, with harsh realities always in sight. Chief among these was that he was still in love with his ex-wife, Lavinia. He never expected that to be otherwise, but the absence of alcohol made these feelings acute. Sometimes he was depressed, and that coupled with the urge to drink, sent him off in his car.

His children were growing up. Angie had turned twenty-one the summer before. Timothy was eighteen and in his last year of high school. The twins, Marta and Maggie, were sixteen and acted it. They thought they knew everything, and Potter found it tiresome. While he was glad that they'd gotten over whatever spat had temporarily separated them, they were a lot to stomach as a pair. Foster was fourteen and still the shy, anxious child he'd always been. He was distinguishing himself academically, and in an accelerated program in the local high school. None of them seemed to need Potter anymore, which made Potter wonder how much they ever had. Lavinia was the one they both fled from and turned to. With her competence and bad temper, she was at the center of their emotional lives, both as the problem solver, and someone to fear. Potter was on the outside and always had been. That was his fault, he knew. He'd spent too much time drinking, and not enough with them.

Sometimes out on the road, he'd stop, lower his window, and invite the cows to low. They took some persuading. Cows were sensitive creatures who always seemed to suspect you meant them harm. Potter cupped his hands to his mouth and mooed long and loud. All he got was a few raised heads, a stare from brown eyes under inky lashes, a steadily chewing jaw that soon lowered back to earth, leaving him forgotten.

He knew the fields well, too. As a boy he'd walked them all. Many were separated by old stone fences that dated from the Revolutionary War. He liked to think he'd find a relic, a button, a piece of torn clothing that would be confirmed as authentic. What he discovered he wouldn't sell but keep forever and think how lucky he'd been to find it at all.

Remembering himself at that age was another unpleasant jolt. He'd had his share of hopes and ambitions then. He never wanted to farm, like his father, and there'd been the usual fights about that. He wanted to go into some kind of business and make money, but he never got a handle on exactly what. Then he met Lavinia and they started a family. She'd had some college under her belt, but didn't finish. To this day he didn't know why. He suspected it was because she hadn't felt up to it. Lavinia used to have an inferiority complex that he tried, without success, to talk her out of. In time he saw that he himself had made that complex worse. How could she think she was capable of high achievements married to a guy who worked odd jobs, couldn't focus on anything in particular, and liked to spend his free time getting drunk?

One Thursday, as a warm sun cleared the last of a sudden spring snowstorm, Potter drove out to his childhood home. A plain Victorian-style farmhouse on five acres, the back portion of which led to a river bottom. Potter's mother used to haul their water from it until the new well was put in. She was a grim, bitter woman with a distant look in her eye that suggested that any time she went out the door she might not come back. She always did, though. Her silence made the house feel cold. Potter remembered that in particular.

Potter pulled his car into the long gravel driveway and got out. There was a *For Sale* sign by the mailbox. He approached the house. Two of the three front steps were broken. The railing along the porch was missing several balusters. One of the two large front windows was cracked. The view through the unbroken one was exactly as Potter remembered. A front parlor with a small fireplace had a doorway at the far end that looked into the kitchen. There were dead leaves on the bare wood floor and cobwebs hanging delicately from the ceiling light.

The back door was unlocked. Potter hadn't thought to try the front. The kitchen floor was a filthy yellow linoleum. The counters were a white laminate flecked with gold. Someone's idea of cheer and happiness, he thought. In his day the kitchen had been an antiseptic white, the only bright room in the house, made brighter by a bare light bulb suspended from the center of the ceiling. In its place now was an opaque fixture rimmed in fake bronze, the kind of thing you bought cheap at the home improvement store.

Potter explored the rest of the downstairs. He stopped at the fireplace. He counted four rows of brick from the bottom on the right, then touched the brick furthest to the wall and wiggled it. It came out in his hand.

"I'll be damned," he said.

In the space was an old snapshot of a girl Potter had been in love with when he was in high school. He couldn't even remember her name. He'd hidden the picture there because he'd carried it in his pocket, and Lavinia was coming by that day. He remembered the picture at the last minute, put it under the loose brick he'd known about for years, then realized he needn't have bothered, because Lavinia would never have known it was on him. He wasn't thinking clearly. Lavinia was coming for a confrontation. He'd lied to her a few days before, and she caught him. They'd gone to a party. He promised to have only two beers. A friend of his let it slip that he'd had five. She was furious and said she wanted to break up. That terrified him. He knew, early on, that he needed her. Her drive was something he could hold on to. Even his parents said that maybe some of Lavinia's shine might rub off on him, if he were lucky. So remembering the picture of the girl he'd loved years before, which he'd made a habit of transferring from pocket to pocket, made him feel both guilty and scared, and he got rid of it at the last minute.

That was the start of everything bad between them, Potter realized. He had trouble telling the truth. Lavinia had no patience. They were less husband and wife than they were accuser and accused. The kids held them together for a long time. Sometimes Potter rose to the occasion. Sometimes Lavinia took a softer tone. But in the end he wore thin and she moved on. He put the picture back where he found it. There was no reason it shouldn't go on sitting in the dark.

The same look of desolation was upstairs, too. The windowpanes hadn't been washed for ages. A rust stain in the bathroom sink would probably never come clean. The room that had once been his had been divided into two smaller ones. The window seat was still there. He lifted the lid. The space below was empty. He didn't know why he thought he'd find the stuffed animals he once kept there. Many people had lived in the house since then. Or, so he assumed.

Later that evening, halfway through his second whiskey, an idea occurred to him. He called Patty long distance.

"Run that by me again," she said.

"I buy the house. I renovate it. I sell it. It's called "flipping.""

"*You've* flipped. You must be drunk."

"I'm not drunk. "

"You're still nuts. What do you know about renovating houses?"

Nothing. He hadn't handled a power tool in years, but he was sure he could learn.

"Besides, who wants to live way the hell out there, even in a really nice house?" Patty asked. She was at her stove, stirring homemade tomato sauce. Murph had requested that she make it. He was having his poker buddies over, and her recipe was a favorite.

"Someone will," Potter said.

They talked a little longer. Patty continued her objections. Potter went on saying he was up to it. And if he wasn't they'd know it soon enough, and in that case she could put the place back on the market. By the end of the call, she had agreed to cosign a loan with him. That's when he confessed that he didn't have a down payment, and would need help with the mortgage.

"Help? You mean you expect me to pay for the whole fucking thing!" Patty threw the wooden spoon she'd used into the sink. Tomato sauce dropped on her newly clean floor.

"I can buy my own tools."

Patty pinched the top of her nose. She often found that it calmed her down.

"You know this means that if I say yes you're only getting the value of your labor," she said.

"How so?"

"Since it's all going to be my money, then I get it all back, minus what I pay you to fix it up. Assuming I don't get my head examined in the meantime."

"Oh." Potter wasn't about to admit that he hadn't thought any of that through. What mattered was that she going to do it, even though she had yet to say so. He knew her well enough to know that if she had her eye on the end result, she was ready to get started.

Because the house was a foreclosure, the previous owners having gotten underwater and moved on rather than be shoved out by the sheriff, Patty had to wait three months for the bank to make up its mind to sell it to her. Potter, acting as her agent, picked up the keys. Then he and his friend Rodney celebrated with a six-pack of beer and a bucket of fried chicken Rodney brought. They built a fire in the parlor. Wood was found around back. Later, the summer night filled with the chirp of crickets. The dark was lit by fireflies. The porch creaked under their boots. Rodney reminisced about the time they tried and failed to jump-start Potter's father's pick-up truck after he refused to let Potter borrow it.

Potter drew himself in tighter. His father was a hard-ass. Gave his smiles out like pennies at Christmas. His touch was still on the place. The narrow windows that were never made wider, and the basement, which was never finished. The one nice thing in the whole house was the dining room, used only on Sundays. That was his mother's pride and joy. If you picked at the wall, which some fool had painted over, you'd see her prize paper. Her big moment. Because his father's cow won something at the fair. And the purse was forty whole dollars.

Enough to hire men to coat the walls. With wide brushes and buckets of sweet-smelling glue. Potter and Patty ordered to stand just over the threshold and watch the sheets lift, sway like sails, and be pressed lightly in place.

Daisies? Jesus, my God, she's gone for daisies!

Patty was sent to her room for saying that. Potter stayed to watch the fields repeat themselves panel by panel. Patty was right. It was all so smarmy. White daisies with their yellow centers. His mother with her arms crossed, wet-eyed, looking on. The men finished their work. She bid them good day and stood rapt. She was walking those bright, crisp fields far from the rough floor that held her soles fast. Dreaming of a world she'd never seen. And that dream was still in her eyes when she finally turned his way. He never forgot how she woke up, looking down at him, as if his very presence had turned that pretty place to dirt.

"Get yourself a steamer. Rents by the hour." Rodney was on his back in the grass, drawing pictures in the air with his blue-nailed finger. He hadn't hurt it working. He'd slammed it in his car door one night coming home from a bar.

"Then what?"

"How should I know?"

Potter didn't like the sound of that. Once again, he got Patty on the phone.

Murph didn't mind. He really didn't. Getting away wasn't so bad. And he happened to have some free time on his hands, which had finally stopped shaking. Murph hated to fly. He'd rather stay on the ground, but the drive out from Helena would have been three days, if he'd taken it easy. And given how easy Murph liked to take things in general, Patty knew those three days would turn into four or five. She bought him a ticket. She even packed his bag. *Go help that sorry-ass excuse for a human being,* is what she told him. Murph was very good with tools and knew just about everything where houses were concerned. Patty never saw why he couldn't make a living as a contractor. But then, that

OUR LOVE COULD LIGHT THE WORLD

would require getting up in the morning on a regular basis, and might put him seriously behind in his drinking.

As to that, Murph told Potter and Rodney that there would be no alcohol on the job. Period. No questions asked.

"Not even a beer with lunch?" Rodney asked. He was a short, round person. In his coveralls, he looked like Humpty Dumpty.

"Nope."

"What about weed? Can we smoke that?"

"No."

Potter was unaware that Rodney smoked pot. He wondered what else he didn't know about him, and about everyone else, really, including his own children, who'd taken the news of his new venture with few comments. The last time he had them all out together, they sat on the picnic bench, ate their burgers, and talked among themselves about people he'd never met, and things that went on at home that he had no knowledge of.

By the end of week one, the place was down to studs. Breathing through a filter made Potter light-headed and Rodney so short of breath he had to go off and sneak cigarettes. Murph threw the debris into the huge, bright green rented dumpster without a word. He had good rhythm. He worked the way a poor man did, steadily and not too fast, knowing that any profit would be small. He'd learned, as Potter had, not to want too much, and to get by with less. He admitted that one night at Lou's over Bourbon shots.

"Patty always wants more," he said. "Not me."

Rodney admired Murph's carpentry skills the most. "Your daddy must have taught you," he said, already tilting in his sturdy chair. Potter liked those chairs. You could drink, and dream, and relive your whole life in a chair that strong. A chair that held you up. Then a chair you could push yourself off of when you had to.

"Didn't have a daddy. Learned it all myself."

"No daddy? What happened to him?" Rodney asked.

"Died."

"How?"

"Got shot."

"Jesus. By who?"

"Cop."

"Get out."

Murph looked at his empty shot glass. His face was still. His bare arms on the table were thick. One had a tattoo of a bird—a dove, Murph had explained when Potter asked him.

"A cop shot him in Billings because he held up a liquor store."

"Jesus. So that's where you're from?"

Murph nodded. "I was eight. Everyone in town heard all about it, and treated me accordingly. Even the pastor of my own fucking church looked me right in the eye as they put his thieving ass in the ground, as if to say flat out that I was, by blood, one sorry piece of shit. And that's when I knew."

"What?" Rodney asked.

"That whatever I learned I'd have to teach myself."

"Here, here." Rodney called for another round. Murph said they'd had enough. Any more, and they wouldn't be able to get up in the morning.

By the end of July, with summer in full swing, the plumbing had been upgraded. So had the wiring. The old windows had been replaced with energy-efficient ones. Potter had to admit that he was learning a lot, working with Murph. He wondered if he could profit by that knowledge down the road, if he ever undertook this sort of project again on his own. With the house livable, Murph moved in and slept on the floor, and cooked his meals on a portable stove he bought with Patty's credit card, the same card that had gotten all their supplies so far. Potter didn't object. Murph had camped out on his couch for over four weeks. He didn't know how Patty felt about his absence. They talked every day at first. Then it fell back to once a week, until it was time to order kitchen appliances. That stuff was spendy, as Murph said, and though Patty had more or less given him an open tab (within reason), he felt the need to consult with her first. She didn't know any more about decorating than he did. She reminded him that they lived in a trailer. She said it wasn't a good idea to show up at the appliance store and let some slick-ass Jack talk through his nose and tell him he what he needed to buy. Potter called Lavinia. He didn't like doing it, but she was their best hope. All the time they'd been married, she'd complained about the kitchens in each of the houses they lived in. Sometimes she outlined exactly what she'd have, if she could. Once they'd gone to a party at a neighbor's place down the block. They were renovating a house that was very much like the one Potter and Lavinia were renting, a Victorian built in the 1880s. The original kitchen was small, fit for only one person to work in at a time. They knocked down a wall and expanded into what had been a small dining room. The result was gorgeous. Lavinia hadn't spoken the whole evening after taking one look at the stainless steel appliances, tile floor, and marble countertops. Potter wondered if that had been the moment when she decided she needed to get out and improve her fortunes elsewhere. Then he didn't think so. Lavinia had never been happy with him. Not after the first few months, anyway.

As he expected, Lavinia didn't appreciate his request.

"You must think I have nothing better to do," she said. The truth was that she didn't. She was tired of playing golf with Chip and his friends. She was tired of the country club. She was tired of the art gallery she occasionally worked in, and the college students who wandered in to escape the heat. She was thinking of going back to school and finally getting her degree. In what, she wasn't sure. Maybe English. She loved nineteenth and twentieth century American novels. She'd been rereading Moby Dick, and though she found she wasn't connecting with it quite the way she had years before, she enjoyed being once more in the grip of the hunter and the hunted.

"It won't take long. Just come and see what we've done," Potter said.

"We?"

"Rodney and Murph are helping me."

"Murph's here?"

"He is."

Lavinia thought back to how Murph had become Chip's drinking buddy three summers before, when Angie was getting out of high school. She thought it best not to mention to Chip that he was in town.

"Oh, all right," she said.

"You know how to get out here?"

"You think I'd forget? I'm not an idiot."

He hadn't thought anything, he was just trying to be helpful. He should have known better. She hung up.

She showed up in a tee shirt and yellow shorts. She wore red flip-flops. With her hair up, she looked about twenty years old. Yet all of her good luck in recent years had made her face harder. She didn't smile once, as if she'd forgotten how. As he watched her circle the kitchen while her shoes made one loud slap after another, Potter had a rare moment of insight—her chronic disappointment had had nothing to do with him. That part of her was a load she brought into their marriage, then carried right on out the other side, only to dump it at Chip's feet. He wished he had a way of telling her that she was the only one, at the end of the day, who could make herself at all happy.

She'd tucked her sunglasses into the neck of her shirt. Her nails were hot pink.

"Not bad. Decent layout," she said.

Murph nodded his appreciation.

"Will the cabinets be custom or stock?" she asked.

"I say probably stock. Patty's starting to breathe down my neck about money. That, and I think she wants me home." Murph grinned. Lavinia sighed.

"Stock's fine, but get the best finish. I say cherry. And make sure the doors are solid, even if the insides are just crappy particleboard," she said.

"Lady knows her cabinets."

Lavinia was continuing her circuit. "Sub-Zero for the fridge. Viking range—six burner. That'll cost you, but it'll be worth it. Copper sink. Carrera countertop. Tumbled glass backsplash," she said.

"Color scheme?"

"Blue and white."

"Classy. Any idea as to the budget here?"

"Forty thousand."

Murph whistled. "I'll have to clear that with the boss," he said.

"You do that."

Lavinia looked around the kitchen once more. The long stare she then gave Murph said she wanted a moment alone with Potter. Murph took himself out back, where Rodney was using his camp stove to heat up some coffee.

"You should have the boys over to see how you're coming along," Lavinia said.

"What for?"

"Because it would be good for them."

"Since when did they get interested in kitchen remodels?"

"Don't be dense, Potter."

What she meant was that Timothy and Foster would have the chance to see their father actually doing something besides cut grass and drink.

"All right, then. Sounds good."

The line between her eyebrows deepened, which meant she was already thinking about something else. On her way out she patted him vaguely on the arm, as if he were just another one of her children.

Patty consented to Lavinia's suggestion. She knew Lavinia had champagne tastes, which might be wasted out there, in the wilds of upstate New York, but she was willing. She had an ulterior motive. When the house was done, she was going to tell Murph to get it professionally photographed, inside and out. That would start his book, the one he'd use to get future clients in and around Helena. She hadn't discussed any of this with him, yet. Better let him get home and have a chance to brag about his feat over a few drinks first.

But the bragging was already underway. Murph showed Timothy and Foster every wall, every seam and joint, every water line and electrical outlet upstairs and down. He described the sanding process that would bring the wood floor back to life. *Your dad wasn't sure we should do it this way,* he often said. *But I convinced him in the end.* There hadn't been any convincing. Potter didn't know how to measure and cut and Murph did. Potter just followed along.

The boys took it in stride. They were bored. Timothy found Murph amusing, and grew curious about how to use various tools. Murph wouldn't let him. He said he didn't want the responsibility. Potter said it was all right, that Timothy had a good head on his shoulders, so Murph showed him how to use the staple gun.

"If it jams, unplug it from the compressor first. Always. No exceptions," Murph said.

Timothy successfully installed a chair rail in the dining room with Murph looking on. Foster, on the other hand, wanted nothing to do with the house or the tools, and spent his time on the back porch where Rodney had made himself quite at home.

"How come you sleep out here? Don't you have a place of your own?" Foster asked him.

"I do. But the old lady has—issues—and I've been enjoying a rare dose of peace and quiet."

Foster agreed that the sounds of the country were soothing. You could sit and hear your own thoughts. It was strange to think that when his father had been his age, he'd lived here, probably sat right where Foster was sitting, and felt what? Foster had no idea.

But Potter had changed, Foster could see that. He moved faster and talked less than before. When Lavinia came to drive the boys home, she asked after him in her veiled way. *Oh, and was your dad helping with that?* and *Really, what did your dad say then?* She always had an eye out for what Potter was doing, even though they'd been divorced six years.

Lavinia had committed her sons to spend a week helping out. By the end of that time, the house was ready for the appliances Murph had ordered. They wouldn't be available for several more weeks, so Murph said he'd take a break, and fly home to keep Patty out of getting into any more trouble than she was already in. Rodney asked if he could go on sleeping on the porch. The August days and nights were pleasant. Potter had no objections to that.

The sense of accomplishment was finer than the best drunk he'd ever been on. He intended to hang on to it, and not let it slip away as so many other things in his life had. He wanted to show off his good work and his dedication, but there was no one who'd appreciate it. Except Angie. She was done with summer school and had free time. He took her out to dinner, which amounted to having burgers by the lake, which she didn't mind.

"How was Timothy's graduation?" he asked.

"Didn't he say?"

"No."

Angie bit down. Thin juice flowed down her small, rounded chin.

"It wasn't anything. I mean, Mom and Chip, they tried to give him a party and he said no. He went off with those friends of his, you know, the Beyers."

"University people."

"Mom's some heavy administrator."

"In the Ag school, right?"

"Knows how to raise those chickens."

Marcia Beyers was the first woman to be promoted in the school of Agricultural Sciences beyond assistant professor. Her real talent was writing and getting federal grants. There was a daughter, Joan, Jane, Potter wasn't sure. Timothy had latched on hard. Potter wondered if he saw himself as a farmer and just hadn't the nerve to say.

Angie said Timothy would be moving out once he started at Dunston University in the fall. Then the make-up of the house would change. She set her chin in her hand when she said this, gazed out of the flat calm water of the lake, and talked about getting a place of her own.

He suggested that she could live in the renovated house through the winter. He didn't intend to put it on the market until spring. People didn't like buying houses in cold weather. He thought he might live there, too, if she didn't mind.

"It's a long commute to school," she said. Being set on the other side of Dunston added fifteen extra miles. She could see Potter's disappointment. She said maybe it would work out, and that she'd give it more thought.

He wanted to drive out and show her around the place. She thought that was fine. The summer twilight was long and pleasant. The leaves were at their thickest this time of year, and made one wavering green wall after another as they rounded all the gentle curves along the way. Yet the blaze was easy to see. First the smoke turned the pale sky black, then the flames lit it up again.

Rodney was in the yard, running back and forth. Fire flowed through the new front windows, and rose towards the soffit Potter himself had nailed in place. There were no nearby neighbors to ask for help, and no cell phone signal either. Had the fire just started, it might have been worth it to race to the closest home, but Potter already knew it was too late for that. The only thing to do now was to stand and watch it burn.

Rodney was leaning on him, clutching at his arm, saying he was sorry, he must have fallen asleep. Both Angie and Potter could smell the liquor on him. Potter thought he must have tossed a tarp aside out back, and it landed on the cook stove that he hadn't turned off. Murph had warned him about using the stove near anything flammable. With Murph away, and Rodney back on the bottle, he'd gotten careless.

They stepped back from the fire's growing heat. The dancing yellow reached the chimney, the one they'd left unchanged because it was still intact. They'd repainted the bricks a fresh bright white, and put in a new mantelpiece. Rodney and Potter hand stained it themselves. As they worked, some stories were shared about a Christmas when Rodney showed up with a plush stuffed bunny for Patty. He'd had a thing for her back in the day. The snap of burning wood was louder.

Emily. That was her name, the girl in the picture. Emily had been the love of his life back then. She was a pretty girl, even prettier than Lavinia. Potter remembered that now.

"Oh!" was all Angie could say. "Oh!"

She dug her fingers into her scalp, then turned and ran towards Rodney who'd fallen to his knees on the grass and was sharing his grief with the starry heavens in long, angry sobs. She helped Rodney stand, and pulled him towards Potter's truck. Potter stayed where he was. It was coming to a head now, and the end was near. He would stay until the roof fell in. He wouldn't be able to bear it after that.

"Come on, Dad! Come on out of here!" In the firelight, Angie looked just like Lavinia, only tougher.

Potter let himself be led. He said nothing. He only wished all this had happened years ago, when he was a solemn, unloved infant too young to remember, or have any sense of loss.

THE ORDEAL

Lavinia didn't like the sound of it. She knew all about their dirty tricks. The whole town did. Some poor kid died every year from an idiotic stunt, just to prove his loyalty. And for what? A fancy place to live with a bunch of alcohol-addled morons.

Chip, on the other hand, was on board. A young man should have a community of peers in which to live and study. He'd had the same opportunity himself, at that age. The memories of chasing women could still make him smile. Chip was dashing, in his day. Or so he believed. Lavinia found his position retarded. Fraternities were trouble, which is why Timothy was drawn to them in the first place, she was sure.

The night Timothy graduated from high school, he'd gotten falling down drunk. Not for the first time. The winter before he came home reeling after a school football game. Lavinia grounded him for two weeks. Chip said she was too harsh. Boys will be boys, he said. She told him he was a cliché. Since then he hadn't overdone it, to the best of her knowledge. But his wanting to join a frat scared the hell out of her. Timothy was like his father, drawn to booze and willing to give up just about anything for the sake of it.

He'd have to maintain a B average, she told him. He sulked at that. He was a poor student, and wouldn't have been admitted at all to Dunston University if Chip hadn't intervened. Secretly Lavinia hoped he'd just flunk out, which would make the matter moot. Then she felt guilty for wishing her own son to fail. She looked at him long and hard, sitting across from her at the table. The way his shoulders slumped, how his hair fell in his face, and that he wouldn't meet her eye, said he'd failed already.

He rushed for the spring semester. The weather was freezing. The wool, button-down coat Chip had bought for Christmas did its job, and gave him an air of sophistication he hoped his future brothers would notice. They did. Also his new shoes, the new car he drove (a Porsche, also courtesy of Chip), the gold watch, and the sneering attitude towards any and all things intellectual. His favorite was Kappa Alpha. They seemed to like him, too. He loved the outdoor deck that wrapped around three sides of the brick building, offering a clear view to Lake Dunston. He stood there, in the plum twilight, stamping snow from his feet and dreaming of the warm days to come, his arm around the thin waist of a sweet, willing girl. A life like that was worth making sacrifices for, he thought, and said so, during his final interview.

He was given a task to prove his worth. He was to take a girl on a date and persuade her to lose her virginity. This necessitated finding a virgin. Timothy didn't see how any of his future frat brothers could know for certain who was, and wasn't, untouched. The answer was easy. There was an on-campus organization of students devoted to the practice of abstinence. They were very public in their declaration that sex before marriage was immoral and against the word of God. Timothy was surprised to find that nut-job evangelicals had managed to penetrate a liberal bastion like Dunston University. There was a girl he would target, one who'd shown interest in the past, only to pull back at the last moment. Her name was Melissa. Timothy would know her at once. She ran their Wednesday Bible Study class and general discussion group. If he liked, Timothy could show up late, so as to skip spending time with scripture. He should appear gentle and pious, open to instruction. What better way to get a girl into bed?

He would prove that he'd done the deed with a small recording device that he could turn off just prior to the act itself, so as to avoid any major embarrassment. Did Timothy feel that he could take on a challenge of this magnitude?

I'm your man, he said.

Then he asked what would happen to the recording. It would be used to blackmail this girl and publicly humiliate her and her cause. One of the brothers worked for the student newspaper. He had an exposé already composed and ready to print. It didn't seem harsh to Timothy.

All's fair in love and war, he said.

He was allowed to move in before the fact. The brothers liked him so much they were willing to bend the rules. His roommate was a big guy from Texas named Joe-Joe. He occupied the outer of two rooms, which meant Timothy had to pass through his anytime he left or returned. Joe-Joe had body odor, farted, snored, and complained that school was too hard. He was a business major. He couldn't grasp the fundamentals of accounting. His father wrote him angry emails about his lack of drive and discipline, which made Joe-Joe drink a great deal of beer. Timothy took Joe-Joe as a necessary inconvenience, a price to pay. As to Timothy's own coursework, he barely paid attention. History of something; Anthropology; Greek Mythology, which he detested; Geology, which he hated a little bit less; and Basic Composition. His body was present in the lecture hall and his mind was on wooing Melissa.

The evening he went to meet her, he lurked in the hall outside the classroom her group used for their instruction. He'd been told to expect a break in between study of the scripture and the discussion. He watched the students file out to use the bathroom or bend over the water fountain. There were two men and four women. Melissa wasn't among them. She'd been described as the only blonde. He peeked through the doorway. She stood at the desk, straightening a stack of papers. She was stunning. Her hair was up. She was slightly built, but curvy in her black turtleneck, tailored slacks, and leather boots. Timothy hadn't expected her to be so elegant. On the desk was a plastic bottle of water from which she took a long drink, her head thrown back. He watched the up and down motion of her throat as she swallowed. He was filled with terror. The girls he went after before weren't like this. They were ordinary creatures with bad skin and crooked teeth who brought their hands to their mouths when they smiled. Timothy couldn't bring himself to join the discussion after the others returned, so he stood another forty-five minutes in the hall and listened to the radiator hiss and thump. When they broke for the evening, Timothy waited a moment, then rushed in and delivered the speech he'd rehearsed in the hall.

"Gosh, did I miss it? I must have gotten the time wrong! That's so dumb of me."

Melissa regarded him coolly. Her eyes were a shade of lavender he'd never seen before. Timothy's face burned.

"Not again," she said. Her voice was smooth and easy.

"What?"

"You frat boys. Give it a rest, already."

She gathered her papers and put them into her backpack. She slipped on her wool coat and pulled a charming wool hat over her ears. She looked about ten years old, ready to throw snowballs.

"I don't know what you're talking about," Timothy said. He'd followed her into the hall at that point.

"Bull. I can spot one a mile away. You guys are a little too slick for your own good, you know that? Now get lost."

She walked away, her boots making a steady *smack, smack, smack* until she reached the stairs. Then she trotted down and he didn't see her.

He wondered if he'd been set up by the brothers. If so, then they were a true bunch of shits. He walked along the sloping path that led from the main quad back to the fraternity. A light snow fell. The night was bitter. At the house, an emergency meeting was underway. One of the brothers had been arrested for drunken driving. Don Bork ("Borko the dorko") was in the city jail, waiting for someone to come and bail him out. Collecting the money wasn't a problem. Convincing his parents to let him remain at Kappa Alpha was. The fraternity's president, Charlie Bainsworth, had a plan. Timothy didn't stay to hear what it was. His venture had dropped down the list of priorities, which was just as well, given that there was no chance he'd be able to go through with it now.

He learned that another brother the year before had made the initial attempt on Melissa, a senior who graduated and left town. She'd blackened his eye, the story went. Timothy had no trouble at all believing that. She looked wiry and strong. He supposed you'd have to be, if you were that pretty and determined to stay a virgin in a college town.

The next time he went to the meeting to wait for her to come out, he invited her for a drink. She stared at him. He was glad she didn't laugh. She asked what made him so dogged. Then she explained that it meant "determined." He was grateful he hadn't had to ask for a definition.

He was shocked that she accepted, though she allowed herself only a diet Coke. Timothy had a beer, then a second. He asked her for her life story. She said she was from Ohio. He said it was a nice place. She asked if he'd ever been there, and he said no.

"Then how do you know it's nice?" she asked. Her sweater had a scoop neck that revealed her collarbone.

"Isn't it nice?"

She laughed.

She didn't ask him anything about himself, which meant she assumed he was like every other guy living in a frat, out for booze and sex. He wanted to prove her wrong and didn't know how. He *did* want to have sex with her. He was also in love, of that he was certain. She'd been the only thing on his mind for weeks. He couldn't tell the guys at the frat about it, obviously. He confided in his brother Foster, however. Foster knew how to keep his mouth shut.

"Tell her, you moron," Foster said.

"It'll scare her off."

"Not if she feels the same way."

"She doesn't."

"How do you know?"

Timothy had no answer. He simply couldn't imagine that his feelings were reciprocated. Or that she'd ever fall for a freshman. Melissa was a junior.

"You're just letting yourself off the hook," Foster said. They were in Timothy's room at the fraternity. Joe-Joe was in class, and they'd spread out into his side of the suite. Foster liked to visit Timothy there. The brothers welcomed him, and no one made fun of his bad leg.

"How am I supposed to say something like that?" Timothy asked. He rifled through the contents of Joe-Joe's desk. He'd found condoms in there before, and took one. Joe-Joe collected rubber bands and paper clips, and small balls of string. Also dead batteries from the game controllers kept in the entertainment lounge. The guy was an idiot, although Timothy was grateful for the stolen condom, which he kept in his wallet.

"Take her out to dinner. Hold her hand. Have a few drinks. It'll be easier than you think, bet you anything." Foster swung around in Joe-Joe's chair until he became dizzy. Timothy drove him home. He thought about what he said. Melissa did seem to like him. He'd taken her out several times. He never tried anything with her, which she had to appreciate. But what if she thought of him only as a friend? It was impossible to know from the way she looked at him. She was always pretty much the same—pleasant, talking about neutral topics, except one time when she said her father was an asshole and didn't follow up with more. She was majoring in economics. Timothy said that was an odd choice. She didn't see why. She was grumpy about it, in fact, and he was sure he'd blown it.

It turned out that her father had discouraged her choice of major on the grounds that it was no field for a woman. *An abstinent woman?* Timothy couldn't help wondering. Her father thought she was wasting her time in college and had refused to pay her way. She was there on a scholarship awarded for her stellar high school record and test scores. Timothy was impressed and said so.

She shrugged. She clearly didn't want to talk any more about herself, so she asked him what it was like growing up in Dunston. He didn't have much to offer. Dunston was a town, much like any other, he supposed. What about his family? What were they like? There he hesitated. He said his mother had remarried a well-off guy who made things possible. His big sister, Angie, was getting her degree in social work from SUNY Cortland. His twin sisters were pretty worthless, and his little brother, Foster, was probably the best of the bunch.

What about his dad?

Timothy held his coffee cup in both hands and thought carefully. He didn't want to scare Melissa off with the truth. He said Potter was between jobs. She didn't ask anything else. She was preoccupied, he could tell.

She wanted to leave all of a sudden. They were in one of the nicer cafeterias on campus. Professors ate there. She barely touched her veal marsala. Timothy had devoured his hamburger. He walked her to her next class. She didn't say a word. He went back to the Kappa Alpha to think.

Joe-Joe was in his boxers playing solitaire on his computer. He wanted to know if Timothy had banged her yet. Everyone in the house was waiting for it to happen, now that Borko the dorko had made bail and calmed his old man down. Timothy said these things took time.

But Timothy didn't think the time would ever be right. She showed no enthusiasm when he kissed her. There was no fire in her eyes when he told her how beautiful she was, or how much he loved her. Those words, which he thought he'd never find, came pouring out the minute he pulled her close. He thought she might laugh at him, or hurt his feelings, but she did neither. He sort of wished she had. Her lack of affect unnerved him.

Foster suggested getting her drunk, not so much to get in her pants, but simply to loosen her up a little. Timothy thought it a splendid idea.

He'd have to find somewhere that didn't ask for I.D. He was underage. She wasn't.

She was the one who solved the problem by inviting him to her place. She lived alone, in a spacious apartment at the back of an old Victorian that had been divided up into separate units years before. The bay window in her living room looked out onto a stand of maple trees that were still bare that time of year. Through the branches, a sliver of lake could be seen, and a sailboat, too. Timothy said that you'd freeze your ass off out there on a day like that. He still had his coat on. She didn't offer to hang it up, so he draped it over the back of the chair that was pushed against her desk, also in the living room.

He'd dressed down, in jeans and an old sweater he hoped gave him a rough, manly air. She'd dressed up in black satin pants and a sleeveless white silk top with thin straps that revealed her small, fine shoulders. He thought she must be miserable, since her apartment was chilly, but her skin was smooth, without goose bumps. She had wine, which she served. She didn't ask if he wanted any. He'd have preferred a beer, but accepted the wine politely. He found it pretty good, actually. She showed him the bottle when he said so. The label meant nothing to him, only that it was French.

She brought a plate of cheese and flat crackers that tasted of garlic. He didn't like the crackers, but enjoyed the cheese. The small napkin she gave him was soon soiled with cheese from his fingers. He didn't know where to put the napkin, so he balled it up when she wasn't looking and stuffed into the pocket of his jeans. She was baking some chicken dish. The aroma filled the room. Suddenly, a tremendous sense of well-being took over. He relaxed.

"Why do you advocate abstinence?" he asked. He didn't think it impertinent, under the circumstances.

"It's a sane policy."

"So, you're a virgin."

Her eyes grew hard as she gazed up at him from her roost on the floor. She sat on a large blue velvet cushion.

"Is that what those fools at the frat told you?" she asked.

"Well, yeah, actually."

"I'm not."

"You're not?"

"And I'm not a hypocrite, either."

"No, of course not."

"I just think people should wait until they're really committed, that's all."

"Right."

"That's why I formed the group. And because I like reading the Bible. I was raised a Baptist, so it's sort of second nature."

He couldn't read her expression.

"There's a lot of it I don't believe, but there's a lot that makes me feel stronger, if you know what I mean," she said.

Timothy didn't know what she meant.

She stood up and said she needed to check the chicken. She didn't want it to burn. She was gone a long time, and he wondered if she'd slipped out, and away from the awkward conversation he'd led her into. The wine was going to his head, and the sense of calm and goodwill gave way to panic. He stood up. The small plate of cheese he'd held on his lap clattered to the floor. She returned, looked at the mess, then at him.

"Sit down, I'll clean it up," she said.

"Ok."

She knelt and picked up the pieces of cheese one by one, put them on the plate, and took the plate to the kitchen. When she came back, she poured him another glass of wine. His heart was pounding. He noticed that her face was flushed. She looked down at him a moment longer. He wondered if he should stand up and kiss her, or pull her down onto his lap. He did neither. She turned away, and went to the window and sipped from her glass.

"Let me explain. I've been wanting to tell you," she said. She was so close to the window that her breath left a small patch of fog. To her, the pane's closeness felt like deep cold. Something she was drawn to.

"I was raped when I was thirteen, by a friend of my father's," she said.

"Oh, man!"

"My father didn't believe me. He said making that kind of accusation could ruin people. This man was a business partner. He'd put a lot of money into my father's company, and my father didn't want him to pull out."

"Unbelievable."

"That's what I said."

She turned around. There were tears in her eyes. She was lovely. Was she asking to be held? He didn't know. He sat still in his chair. She wiped her eyes and said dinner was nearly done.

After she had a lot to drink, she took him into her bedroom. She was laughing, and unsteady on her feet. She swayed into him. Her skin was warm. She stripped, and lay naked on her bed, giggling. Timothy got undressed and lay down beside her. She closed her eyes and mumbled something about the dinner they'd just had, which he'd enjoyed a lot. He didn't know why she was thinking about that now. Her bedroom was cold, and he got under the covers. There were cracker crumbs in her bed. She went on lying as she had, flat on her back, eyes closed, a gentle smile on her face. Then she was asleep.

Timothy turned over on his side, with his back to her. He remembered her refilling her glass, then opening another bottle of wine as they ate. She drank faster than she had when the evening began. It was as though she wanted to make herself numb in order to sleep with him. She couldn't face it sober. Maybe that wasn't his fault at all, but the memory of her ordeal. That idea didn't comfort him much. He wanted to wake her up and make her fuck him. That would be wrong, though. She'd end up hating him.

The moonlight fell on her wood floor. He got up, got dressed, wrapped her in the portion of quilt he'd lain under, and left.

It was past midnight when he reached the house. Joe-Joe was up and staring at his computer screen. He turned his thick head towards the door when Timothy came in. His eyebrows shot up to ask how the evening had gone. Timothy hesitated. Then he gave a thumb's up and went quickly into his own room.

The following day, Sunday, the brothers plied Timothy for information. He said it would be ungentlemanly to provide any details. They seemed to have forgotten all about using a recording device to support his claim. Timothy didn't, and covered himself by saying he'd forgotten to bring it to her place, because he'd had no idea that she would want to seduce him. He'd given up, in other words, and had more or less accepted the platonic nature of their relationship. That caused a number of snickers and grins. One guy asked if it hurt her, because it was supposed to hurt the first time. Timothy said she gave nothing away. Later, he congratulated himself on his witty reply.

He stopped congratulating himself when Melissa didn't want to see him again. She wasn't exactly embarrassed by what had happened, the bulk of which she remembered, but she realized from her behavior that she was incapable of having a serious relationship at this point in her life. She said it would always be an issue, not just with him, but with any guy, and she obviously couldn't handle it, because of what she'd been through. She needed time to sort herself out. Timothy asked how much time. She said she didn't know and hung up the phone.

He confessed everything to Foster. Foster said it was too bad, but probably best all around. The girl was clearly a nutcase, and Timothy should consider himself lucky to be rid of her. He also said Timothy should be grateful that he'd had to perform such an easy feat to be accepted by the brothers, as opposed to say, swallowing goldfish, or cramming himself into a phone booth with fifteen other people. Timothy thought Foster got those ideas from old movies since no one did those things anymore. One tradition that held fast, though, was hitting the bottle in times of stress. The ordeal with Melissa made Timothy turn to beer, then to vodka, and spend the better part of a month totally plastered.

He failed his classes and didn't care. He stayed away from campus entirely to avoid Melissa. When he was particularly down, and not too drunk to manage his phone, he sent plaintive text messages, *please*, and *one more chance*, and then finally, *I love you*. That last one got a response. *I'm sorry*, she wrote, as if loving her were an illness or accident, or maybe something she had to apologize for. He sat in his room and wept. Word went around that he'd been dumped. Sympathy flowed from the brothers. Women were bitches. They never knew when they had a good guy. They all wanted losers and jerks. He was better off without her.

Blind dates were suggested. A number of girls were introduced at house parties. None had her sparkle. None even came close. Timothy sank lower and lower into himself, so that some days, now that spring had come, he was shocked to see the sun shine.

He moved back home. Lavinia suspected he'd drunk himself out of school and was furious. Chip, though not furious, was grim and condescending. Young men needed to learn limits, he said. Fun was fun, and work was work. Everything in moderation, he said. Timothy despised him. He was sure Chip had never been in love, not even with his mother, because he found the notion impossible to entertain.

Foster told him to get a grip. Melissa was just a girl, after all, and the world was full of them. Timothy told Foster he didn't know his ass from his elbow. Then he said that at fifteen, Foster didn't know shit about love, or anything else, for that matter. Foster was hurt. He'd tried to be there whenever Timothy needed him. Now he'd have to make it on his own, without his help, because he wasn't about to be insulted by his own brother.

So Timothy sulked. He stayed up all night and slept all day. In the morning, Lavinia found the evidence of how he'd spent his time while the rest of the household slept. There were pizza boxes, empty beer cans, overdue DVDs from the rental place in the shopping center, charges on her credit card for gas and clothes he bought and didn't wear. She sat him down and asked what the hell was wrong with him. He told her to leave him alone. She got the scoop from Foster, who said

Timothy had girl trouble. She approached him again, this time more gently. She said everyone falls in love and gets turned down. It was all a part of growing up. When he looked at her, his eyes were raw and full of pain. She saw a much younger Timothy then, the little frightened boy he'd once been, and when he wept suddenly, with a great show of energy and despair, the years between then and now disappeared. She took him in her arms and held him until he calmed.

THE CAREGIVER

He talked in terms of before and after. Before his wife died, he was a little overweight. Afterwards he lost twenty pounds without even trying. Before he had a vegetable garden out back. They ate the tomatoes and lettuce all summer long. Beanstalks this tall, he said, lifting his thick, weathered hand. Afterwards the garden went back to nature. He talked as if he'd known all along that life was a losing battle. Frank LaVelle had about as much misery as someone could have, Angie thought. So much that he didn't even know he was miserable. He just muddled through as best he could. Only he couldn't very well now, which was why she was sitting with him in his tiny, filthy kitchen, while a white cat, one of three that lived there, circled her feet and purred. The house stank of garbage. His daughter had made the call. *Someone needs to look in on my father,* she said. The daughter lived, as the crow flew, two miles away. And she couldn't do the looking in. But Angie wasn't quick to think less of her. It wouldn't be easy, seeing what grief had reduced your father to.

Angie knew that firsthand. After Potter's house burned down two years ago, he fell apart. He stopped sleeping. Then he stopped eating. The fact that he didn't take a drop of liquor worried Angie the most. His eyes took on a focused, unseeing look, as if something in his head was speeding out of control. His sister, Patty, was still paying off the bank loan. She didn't complain about it to Potter as far as Angie knew. Rodney, the guy Potter had been working with on the house, disappeared. Just left town, and no one knew where or heard from him after that. Potter worked at the home improvement store. He'd learned a thing or two in the course of his renovations. He drove the forklift around the back lot when deliveries came in. Management was considering him for a sales position. He was always neat and trim. Steady on his feet, too. With that disturbing look that no one but Angie seemed to notice.

Angie wanted to arrange for a home care aide to visit Mr. LaVelle twice a week.

"She'll shop for you and help you with your housework," she said.

"My daughter does all that."

Angie knew that the daughter hadn't been inside the house in over four months. She gave him a little money from time to time. She handed it to him through the screen door in back.

"Yes, of course. But I imagine her job keeps her pretty busy." The daughter worked for the university in the payroll department. She had regular hours and no family, but it seemed like the right thing to say.

"She's the best daughter a man could ask for."

"Sure sounds like it."

The cat continued its circuit. Then it jumped into Mr. LaVelle's lap. It nuzzled the front of his stained, plaid shirt.

"Isn't she a pretty one? Guess I still have a way with the ladies," Mr. LaVelle said.

Mr. LaVelle stroked the cat's head. His fingernails were black. Angie thought it best to let the aide tackle that particular problem. Angie already had someone in mind. Marcy Brockman. She was a retired math teacher, mentally sharp and physically fit. If anyone could straighten up Mr. LaVelle's house—and persuade him to take a shower regularly—she could. Marcy was a temporary measure, though. Soon enough Mr. LaVelle would have to move into a group home.

"I'll bring a friend with me next time," Angie said. "She's going to take a look around and make a few suggestions."

"She doesn't have to do that."

"I know. But you'd be doing me a favor. She's sort of at loose ends."

"How come?"

"Well—her kids are all grown. She's got time on her hands."

"No husband?"

"Divorced."

"Pretty?"

"You stop that."

Angie rose to go. It amazed her sometimes how easily she could tell someone what he needed to hear.

Potter spoke quietly out of consideration for Angie's boyfriend, Brett. Brett was a graduate student in economics. He slept a lot when he wasn't studying. He was sleeping again when Potter came by. Potter watched Angie slice carrots for the soup she was making and said he'd been evicted from his apartment several weeks before and had been living in his pick-up truck ever since. *Maybe you could see me clear. Probably best not to tell your landlord, though.* Chip owned the house. A small place, set on a cul-de-sac, backed by a wall of trees. Quiet. Private. Peaceful. A place where Potter could hear himself think. There'd been tenants in there before who moved away and skipped the last two months of their rent. Chip considered selling it, but the market was still soft, so he offered it to Angie. She refused to live there for free and paid him the going rate on time every month. Potter was proud of her for that. He was also proud of her job with the County Department of Social Services. The boyfriend he wasn't sure about. He seemed a little too slick for his own good, someone who pretended to be independent and still needed his hand held.

Angie said it wouldn't be convenient, but that they'd make it work. She didn't ask how long he needed to stay. The second bedroom was tiny and Potter didn't mind. Everything he owned was already in his truck, and it took little time to get settled.

Brett surfaced around one in the afternoon. Potter was at the table, drinking coffee. He said he'd moved in. He hoped Brett was okay with that. Brett's face tightened, and the color rose in his cheeks. He wanted to give Angie a quick call at work.

"Don't. She's busy," Potter said.

"She might have asked me."

"Didn't want to wake you up."

"Still."

"She pays the rent, doesn't she?" Potter knew Brett contributed nothing. He was in school full-time and his resources were stretched, or so he said. There was a nice car in the driveway and a new motorcycle in the garage, both of which were his. Some people had a different concept of poverty, Potter thought.

"My house, too," Brett said.

"Yeah. How you figure that?"

At that Brett left Potter alone. In front of Angie they were polite. When it was just the two of them in the house, which wasn't often because Potter was working regularly and Brett had class, they didn't speak.

Brett talked to Angie, instead. His voice took on a whiny tone it didn't have before.

"He stinks up the bathroom," Brett said. It was evening, and they were home alone. Potter had gone out, probably to give them some space, Angie thought.

"So do you."

Brett sipped his tea. He was a passionate tea-drinker. Angie found it affected. She used to like it. They'd met in the grocery store. She'd pulled a Yukon gold potato from near the bottom of the heap, because it was the plumpest and nicest looking, and the others above it rolled onto the floor. He came to the rescue. He was painfully handsome with wild, bushy blond hair. He seemed disciplined and hard-working, yet was vulnerable, too, and openly sought affection. He had a sense of humor that wasn't always kind. He teased her often about the potato. It came to represent something about her in his mind, blind faith at times, or when he was peeved, a sad lack of judgment. It was the lack of judgment he promoted now.

"You're doing his laundry," Brett said. His eyes were a deep blue that reminded Angie of her former professor.

"So? I did it all the time before they split up."

Brett knew about Angie's childhood. In the beginning, he'd been charmed by it. His own background seemed so ordinary by comparison. He was an only child. His parents were still married. His father was a plastic surgeon in Minneapolis. His mother taught school.

"How long is he going to stay?" Brett asked.

"I told you, I don't know and I don't care."

"You should give him a deadline."

"No."

"Then I will."

"I wouldn't, if I were you."

The set of her there in the doorway to their bedroom and the black suit she'd worn to work told Brett not to push it. She was the most stubborn person he'd ever known.

"All right, all right. But I *hate* the way he looks at me," Brett said.

Angie knew Potter couldn't stand Brett. She also knew he'd never say so. They had always been like that, she thought. Aware of each other's truths without needing to say much. Brett was the opposite. He was clueless and talked all the time, always about himself.

The light bulb in Mr. LaVelle's kitchen burned out. The ladder was in the basement and too heavy to bring upstairs. Mr. LaVelle went to his back porch. On one wall he had piles of magazines and newspapers. On another wall was a stack of old telephone books, some dating back twenty years. His wife had hated those the most. *Why keep them? You never call anyone, anyway.* She did the calling. The inviting. The hosting. Such a bright place, the house had been back then. Mr. LaVelle brought out six books. He had to make two trips. He put them, one atop another, neatly below the light bulb. He climbed up, out of breath. As he reached for the dark bulb, the books shifted and he fell. He didn't think he blacked out. No time seemed to have been lost. Marcy found him sitting on the floor, looking cross, like a little boy, she told Angie. That was very near the truth, Angie thought. Some elderly people became childish once again, as if life followed a loop, not a straight line.

The furnace stopped working the following week, and since it was just early spring, the cold gathered in the small house. Rather than call for a repairman, Mr. LaVelle turned on his gas oven, hauled his recliner into the kitchen, and used it as a bed. Once again, Marcy reported that in her opinion, Mr. LaVelle had significant challenges living on his own. The house was cleaner, thanks to her, but Mr. LaVelle had refused her help in the matter of personal hygiene. She managed to wash his clothes and towels, but the frequency with which he bathed dropped to twice a week.

"Finally I had to tell him flat-out that he smells," Marcy said.

"You shouldn't have done that."

"No choice."

Angie could see then what sort of a teacher she'd been. But it worked. Mr. LaVelle still had enough pride to be embarrassed at having offended her, and he showered every morning. Shaving he needed to be reminded about. Marcy realized he never looked in the mirror.

"That's another sign he's not all there," she said.

Angie wasn't so sure. Mirrors were harsh. She herself had always hated them. Especially before she lost weight. She'd kept most of it off, which she found easier to do if she didn't have to confront her own image very often.

She told Marcy to continue as she had, that Mr. LaVelle would stay put for the moment. Then she put in a call to the Brookside Group Home to see if they might have any availability in the next one to two months.

〜

Brett went to Minnesota for spring break. Angie figured he needed some time without Potter breathing down his neck. He'd stayed in the background at first, but over the passing weeks, she found him watching Brett more closely, even suspiciously. She was annoyed and told him so. She reminded him that it wasn't easy for Brett having him there, and that everyone was trying to make the best of it.

"Do you want me to move out? In another few weeks I'll have enough money for a deposit on another place. Trouble is, anyone checks my references . . . well, you know. I could ask Patty to back me up, but she did that once already," he said. Patty called every week to see how Potter was getting along. She asked after Angie, too. Angie didn't send her emails anymore. At home, the computer was Brett's and at work, she didn't think it was appropriate. "Could always ask your mom, but I value how firmly rooted my teeth are."

"You don't need to move out, Dad. It's all good. You just make Brett nervous, that's all," she said.

"Maybe he's got a guilty conscience."

"Right."

Potter said nothing about the phone calls Brett made when Angie wasn't home, or the sexy voice he used, or the way he looked pleased with himself afterwards. He could keep secrets as well as the next guy, but he sure as hell didn't like to.

Three days later, Potter saw Brett's Lexus climbing Boundary Drive from downtown. Potter was on his lunch break, running an errand for his boss. Potter followed the car another four blocks to a house just off campus where Brett parked, got out, and was met by a tall, blonde-haired girl in very tight pants. Their embrace was more than friendly. Potter drove off before he was seen.

Brett played it well. He called Angie every day from his cell phone and described having dinner out with his folks, how strange it was to be home, fleshing out his lie with loving details. Angie's face was softer when she got off the phone with him. Potter's heart was harder. Still he kept silent. He smiled when she said funny things about her day.

He feigned interest in Mr. LaVelle, who was holding his own, Angie said. She described running into the daughter one day on her way out. Looking back from her car, Angie saw Mr. LaVelle in the doorway, talking to her through the screen door.

"Place is all picked up now. Don't see why she can't go on in," Angie said.

"Maybe he won't let her."

"Why wouldn't he let her?"

"People get strange notions."

They were eating dinner. Potter had treated them to takeout Chinese food. The place he got it from took him by Brett's love nest. The car was there, parked in a different spot from where it had been. Bastard probably needed to go out for beer, Potter thought. Or condoms. He hoped to hell he was using condoms. Last thing Angie needed was some STD.

Angie considered the peapod squeezed between the ends of her chopsticks. She looked grim. Potter was afraid she'd say she missed Brett and couldn't wait for him to return. He was awfully glad she didn't.

Mr. LaVelle ran himself through the multiplication tables every morning over coffee. He did the crossword puzzle. He listed states and their capitals he'd memorized as a boy. Since there was no one else in the house to ask, he didn't know if his unspoken answers were correct or not. He wished the cats could talk. Sometimes they did, late at night, when he was trying to sleep. They always discussed his late wife, though only one of them had known her.

"She loved honey," the tabby said. "On her toast. In her tea. There was even some recipe—pork glazed in honey—that she loved to death."

"Maybe that's what killed her," the black one said.

"You're rude!" That was the white female. They'd all had names before giving them up. Mr. LaVelle didn't know when they'd decided to become anonymous. He thought it had something to do with his forgetting what he once called them. They probably got sick of going by "kitty."

Marcy reported that Mr. LaVelle said the cats needed to be put in another room overnight because they kept him up.

"That sounds reasonable. Cats are nocturnal. They probably roam around and get into things," Angie said.

"They're talking."

"Say again?"

"He says they're talking. As in the English language. Long conversations."

"Oh."

"Maybe we should get a psych profile worked up on him?"

"I'll get on it first thing tomorrow."

Angie forgot to because Brett called her the night before to say he had big, big news.

"My dad's sending me to Europe for three weeks this summer. Isn't that great?" he said.

"Fab."

"You don't sound very excited."

"I'm not."

"Really?"

"Really."

A woman laughed in the background. Brett had said he was calling from a restaurant in Minneapolis. Angie wondered why he was eating so early. It was five-thirty in Dunston, and Minneapolis was two hours behind.

"Well, maybe this will get you moving. While I'm gone, you can make plans," Brett said.

"What plans?"

"How about a wedding?"

"Are you shitting me?"

"Isn't that what you wanted?"

She never said she did.

"When did you decide all this?" she asked.

"Today. Just now. Isn't it great?"

She didn't know. She couldn't seem to muster the smallest glow in her heart.

"I have to go. I have another call. It's probably my dad," she said.

"Oh, him. What's *he* going to say about this?"

"I haven't the slightest idea."

"Doesn't matter, really. As long as he doesn't live with us when we're married."

Angie hung up. *What the fuck,* she thought. *What the fuck?*

On the night before Brett was due home, Potter stayed up late and left the house quietly around one-thirty in the morning. He parked a block from Brett's girlfriend's house. There were no lights on. He stabbed each of the brand-new tires on Brett's sports car with an awl. The third puncture set off the car alarm. The house remained dark, and Potter assumed everyone inside was dead drunk. He was grateful that the house stood far back from the road. He scratched the word "cheat" on the hood while the alarm went on sounding. The front door opened. The girlfriend was standing there, buck-naked. Potter admired her tits. It had been a while since he'd seen a pair. He was in the shadows, and he knew she wouldn't come down the steps without any clothes on. She turned and looked behind her, back into the light she'd come out of, and he sprinted up the driveway. Safe in his truck, he grinned. Then he laughed. At Angie's, it took a long time to get to sleep. When he did, it wasn't for long, because Angie woke him up. She sat on the end of his bed. She was crying.

"He asked me to marry him," she said.

"Jesus. When?"

"Few days ago. He hasn't called since. I'm worried. I must have pissed him off."

"Why?"

"Because I didn't say yes."

"So you said no."

"I didn't say anything."

Potter sat up and ran his fingers through his thinning hair. For the first time in ages, he wished he had a drink.

"What are you going do?" he asked.

Angie shrugged. The room was lit with a thin sliver from the setting moon. She made a gooey noise in her throat.

"I can't marry someone like that," she said.

"Like what?"

"He just not . . . there."

Potter wasn't sure what she meant.

"He spaces out? Loses track?" he asked.

"There's just something missing. Like there's a big hole inside of him. And I keep getting pulled down inside of it. Like it's swallowing me up." Angie used the back of her hand to wipe her nose. "I feel like he's always counting on me. Like he needs me."

"He's a big boy."

"He's not though, don't you see? That's the problem."

Potter sat up with his pillow pressed behind his back.

"*His* problem. You make it yours, one day you'll wish you hadn't." That was the closest Potter had ever come to giving his daughter advice.

"Go back to bed. Take tomorrow off. Give yourself a break," Potter said.

"Can't. Wrapping up Mr. LaVelle."

"Yeah? What's his deal?"

"Moving him into a group home."

"Bet he won't go quietly."

"Bet you're right."

She went on crying. He couldn't tell if it was about Brett, Mr. LaVelle, or life in general. He walked her back to her own room, then made himself a pot of coffee. There was no way he would sleep now.

Angie cleaned the house. She made pot roast. She wasn't a very good cook, but she tried hard. She put her hair up and wore eyeliner. Watching her made Potter want to put his fist through a wall. Brett arrived in a car she didn't recognize. She stood on the porch to greet him, looking just like a loving wife.

"What's this?" she asked.

"Rental. Someone messed up my Lexus."

"Tough neighborhood out there, eh?" Potter asked. Brett looked at him crossly.

"You mean it was vandalized?" Angie asked.

"Yup."

"That's terrible!"

"Real shame," Potter said. Brett went past him, carrying his pack. Potter let them eat dinner alone, because Angie had asked him to beforehand. He took another drive, this time out in the county. He was tempted to swing by the house that burned down, and knew he didn't have it in him yet. Patty still owned the land it had sat on. Maybe he could persuade her to let him build another house there, in time. A smaller place that would be comfortable for one or two people. In his heart, he imagined living there with Angie, though he knew it wasn't the best thing for her. She needed to go on with her own life. A life absent from Brett. He hoped to hell she wasn't going to change her mind about marrying him. A man like that would never be anything but trouble.

On the way back into town, Potter turned onto the avenue where Brett had spent his vacation. He pulled into the driveway. The damaged car was still there. He turned off his engine, got out, and knocked on the door. The sound of music was clear. He knocked again. The door opened, and the woman he'd seen nude a few nights before looked down at him.

"Yes?" she said.

"Brett sent me." Potter's heart picked up speed.

"What's that lying fuck want?"

"Um, well, he says he's sorry."

The woman stared down at Potter with narrow eyes. She was nicely dressed, with gold jewelry on her wrists and neck.

"He could have told me that himself. That loser never could his pull own weight, though. Figures he'd send a go-between," she said. She looked sad, all of a sudden, and Potter wondered if he might have a chance with her. He was a good twenty years older than she was, but he was in great shape. People told him so all the time.

"Tell him I'm having the car towed. I thought you were the tow guy, in fact," she said.

"I look like a tow guy?"

She stared at him. "How do you know Brett, anyway?" she asked.

"Mutual friend."

Potter tipped his baseball cap and left her still standing in the doorway. He wondered what was going on back home, what garbage Brett was telling Angie. Brett reminded Potter of a guy he once knew on the campus grounds crew. Had women stashed all over town, and since Dunston wasn't that big a place, eventually someone got wise. Either Brett was really, really stupid, had blind faith in luck, or wanted to get caught. Some men made a career of fucking up, then asking for forgiveness. He hoped to hell Angie was too smart for that, but then, she'd taken up with him in the first place.

At the house Brett was the only one there.

"She went to the liquor store. Wanted a bottle of champagne," Brett said. He was at table, with most of the food left on his plate.

"You celebrating something?"

"Sort of."

Potter pulled up a chair. "Is it what I think?"

Brett put his elbows on the table. He brought his chin up, like someone used to having center stage.

"We've come to a parting of the ways," he said.

"Oh. Doesn't usually call for champagne."

"Angie's got an odd sense of humor. Bet she gets that from you." His tone had an edge. "She thinks we should be glad that we avoided, how did she put it, a 'grievous' mistake.'"

"She upset?"

"More like relieved."

Potter could see that Brett was genuinely hurting. *Idiot*, he thought. Potter got himself a serving of Angie's pot roast. It wasn't bad. A lot better than Lavinia used to make, but then Lavinia had no patience. She always boiled the meat. Meat was something you couldn't boil.

He finished eating. Brett hadn't said a word.

"Let me ask you something, man to man," Potter asked.

Brett's chin was as high as it had been before.

"How come you asked her to marry you? What is it you figured she'd be getting?"

"What are you talking about?"

"Angie deserves better than some half-assed two-timer."

Brett looked hard at Potter. He flushed.

"I don't know what you mean," he said.

"Yes you do, so cut the crap."

Brett said nothing. His face turned pinker.

"You spent your vacation with a woman on College Avenue. A good-looking woman, at that," Potter said.

"You had me followed. I knew it. The way you look at me."

"No. I just saw you driving one day when you were supposed to be in Minnesota."

Brett finished his cup of tea. It smelled dark and earthy, like mulch. Potter couldn't stand it.

"She's pretty pissed at you, by the way," Potter said.

"You talked to her? Why?"

"Hey, shithead, I'm asking the questions here."

"Fuck you."

"Fuck you, too. Now spill it."

Brett's eyes got wet. He seemed to collapse in on himself. The last man Potter saw cry was Rodney, after he burned down Potter's house.

"Take it easy. Just trying to get to the bottom of things," Potter said. He wished he had that drink, the one flashing in the corner of his eye for the longest time.

"Sheryl was my girlfriend before Angie," Brett said. His nose was drippy. He looked about five years old. "I went to see her."

"Why?"

"I wasn't happy with Angie. She's—distant."

"What the hell does that mean?"

"She can be cold. And keep to herself."

"You trying to say she doesn't put out the way you want?"

"No!"

"But you went back to mama to see if there was some honey left in the pot."

"You're a crass old fart."

"And you're a douchebag."

Brett wouldn't meet Potter's eye. His center of gravity shifted towards the surface of the table, as if it were pulling him in.

"I thought, well, I thought that I'd give it one more try. You know, with Sheryl," he said. His voice was ragged.

"And?"

"She turned me down."

"You proposed to her, too? Jesus Christ." Brett stared into his empty mug. Potter wondered how much Angie would mind if he beat the shit out of him, then and there. *Take it easy,* he told himself.

"Okay, then what happened?" Potter asked

"I told her about Angie."

"Dumbass!"

"I was upset. I wanted to hurt her."

"Which you did, but then you found yourself without a lifeboat, so you came crawling back." A car approached. They listened. It went on down the road.

"You're not worth the half of her. And given what I know, it's real, *real* lucky for you she didn't say yes," Potter said.

Brett sat in silence. His wet eyes looked at nothing. His breathing slowed, then he got up, took his tea cup out, and washed his face at the kitchen sink. Angie's car came into the driveway. Once again, Potter left them alone. The way he'd been having to make himself scarce lately, he might as well have been living on his own.

With Brett gone, Angie's spirits were good, though at times she sagged, growing moody and silent. Mr. LaVelle moved into the group home. When they went through the house, they found that two of the three cats were dead. It seemed that Mr. LaVelle had slit their throats. Angie was at a loss. Marcy reported that Mr. LaVelle continued to insist that the cats were talking late into the night, keeping him awake. He said he was sorry about it, that he hadn't wanted to do it, but that the cats left him no choice. Only the white female cat remained, and Angie took him to live with her and Potter. Brett called. He wanted Angie to reconsider. She said she'd done all the considering she was going to do.

Brett called another day. Angie was in the shower. Potter answered her phone, which was lying in the middle of her carefully made bed.

"Oh, it's you," Brett said.

"Surprise."

"Yeah? Well I've got a surprise for you."

"What?"

"I know you did it."

"Did what?"

"My car. I know you wrecked my car."

"And what exactly do you think that knowledge is worth?"

Brett hung up and didn't call again.

One night, when Potter worked a double shift to cover for a guy whose baby was sick, Angie stayed home with the cat, which she still hadn't named. It slept in her lap, and woke when she stroked its soft, smooth head. She asked it if she'd ever find the right man, one who'd give a little more than he'd take. The cat said nothing, only purred and looked at her with pure love in its green eyes.

LAVINIA

She told the girl at the flower shop that her name was Lavinia Dugan. She'd been Lavinia Starkhurst for years. How could she have forgotten that? And why had the past suddenly laid its claim? She was there to order arrangements for her former sister-in-law's wedding. A generous act by any standard. She didn't like Patty one bit and never had. When she got the news of her engagement, Lavinia sneered. Patty was a fool. That true love lay in her heart Lavinia ignored. *Love, shmove*, she thought. Yet, on some level, she knew it had to be so. Why else would Patty bother to marry Murph now, after all these years? Surely it wasn't because he knocked her up. Patty was Lavinia's age— late forties was as specific as Lavinia would get on that point. No, it was some odd softness that she must have discovered in a weak moment. Maybe she was ill, and her days were numbered, but that seemed unlikely. Patty, like Lavinia, was of sturdy stock, and essentially too tough for any disease to take hold.

Lavinia told the idiot girl behind the counter that she wanted one large centerpiece of white roses and white carnations, no added greenery, and to go light on the baby's breath. The girl chewed her gum, broke the tip of her pencil, and stared crossly at it. Lavinia dug a pen out of her purse and gave it to her. She also wanted two smaller vases to go at either end of the long table she was renting. Both would have white roses and lilies, not carnations. The table would stand in Lavinia's front hall, contrary to Patty's wishes. It was summer, and Patty was coming in from Montana to get married in her hometown. She wanted an open-air ceremony and reception. Lavinia couldn't believe that Patty had forgotten what June in Dunston could be like. Unpredictable, to say the least. Lavinia wasn't about to stand around in drizzle.

The girl gave Lavinia her receipt. Lavinia noticed that she'd written down the wrong telephone number. She asked her to correct it. The girl crossed it out, which left no room on the form to fill in the right one, so she had to start the paperwork all over again. Lavinia waited, awash in the scent of fresh flowers, something that used to bring her joy and now only made her sad.

At home, Chip sat in his study with a drink and gazed out the window at the sloping, emerald grass of his back lawn. Lavinia greeted him by patting his head, something she used to do to her dog when she was a little girl. The memory struck her, and she returned to plant a dry kiss on his cheek, which she hoped he'd appreciate. He didn't seem to notice. He wanted to know how her day had been.

"Busy. Frustrating. Not very successful," she said. After the florist's, she went by the caterer's. A thin, nervous young man with bad skin outlined his plan. Heavy hors d'oeuvres, he said. Pear and brie tartlets, roasted vegetables with a tomato basil dipping sauce, lamb sliders with caramelized onions. Lavinia reminded him that she wanted a menu for a sit-down dinner. She wanted everyone to be served, not to have to fend for themselves. The young man sighed, and said he'd look over his notes from their initial conversation and have a new proposal for her within two days.

Lavinia didn't ask how Chip's day had gone. His days were very much the same. Since spraining his ankle badly last year, he couldn't play golf. Golf had kept him going. Now whiskey kept him going, along with a keen interest in Lavinia's doings. Patty's wedding was a source of great fascination for him. He offered opinions and advice. Lavinia couldn't stand it. That was why she'd forgotten her last name, she decided. Chip was driving her nuts.

When she was really honest with herself, often to the point of soul searching, usually late at night when sleep eluded her, she called herself a liar. Chip was just Chip, only a little more so now that he had time on his hands. Chip wasn't the problem. Her stupid heart was. The truth was she didn't love him and never had. She'd tried a long time to make the best of it. She married him for his money—not a trivial concern for someone with five children, to be sure, but still not the best basis for a happy future. She still valued the money. It was impossible not to. And it wasn't bad to have someone to sit with in the evenings, now that the children had their own lives. The twins still lived at home but were often out, either together or separately. Each had her own set of friends. Maggie's group went to concerts a lot. Marta's cruised the mall. Timothy was around from time to time. He had an apartment in College Town that Chip paid for after Lavinia told him she couldn't have him under her roof any longer. Timothy was sullen and resentful, wishing the world would give him some unspecified reward just for being in it. Then there was Foster, as sweet and anxious as ever. His limp had gotten worse. No one seemed to know why. Lavinia guessed that he exaggerated his awkward gait on purpose, as if to say that he might be crippled, but it would never slow him down.

She loved Ethan, Chip's son. Or she had, at the time, a few years ago. Or so she thought. She no longer had those feelings for him, only the memory of them and how they drove her crazy. Chip never suspected. Or if he did, he didn't let on. She would have denied it, if confronted. She would have said she never wanted a physical relationship, that she cherished her marriage, when in fact she wanted very much to sleep with Ethan and would have dumped Chip in a heartbeat if Ethan had been receptive. Ethan might have been receptive, if the idea of taking on five children hadn't scared him off. The one and only time he wrote her after he went back to California, he mentioned her children. *You must consider their welfare,* were his very words. The letter followed the one phone call she made to him in desperation. She had actually wept. She threw herself at him over all those miles, and begged him to open his heart to her. He wouldn't. *I don't feel that way about you. I'm sorry.* She actually considered killing herself, rather than carry the agony of his rejection for the rest of her life. The part of her that was wise said she was being foolish and to just wait it out. It took well over a year, but the wound finally healed.

Lavinia realized she wasn't going to fall back asleep anytime soon. The nighttime wakefulness was more and more frequent. Hormones, she assumed. The beginning of the change. Chip slept solidly. That was probably why he drank so much, so he could pass the night as though it were a blank interval between the end of one day and the start of the next. He wasn't happy with her. She knew that. He was committed, though. She knew that, too. He wouldn't walk out. He wasn't the walking out kind. Lavinia was. No matter how much she told herself otherwise, she now understood that when the time seemed right, she'd tell Chip she wanted a divorce.

And then what? Evenings on her own, that's what. Days on her own, too, since she didn't work anymore.Chip would let her stay, even if they had separate bedrooms. That seemed cold, though. Colder than a clean break.

By the time she got downstairs and helped herself to a large whiskey in Chip's study, she knew she'd never leave him. She was too comfortable. Even if she met someone and fell in love, she doubted she'd be able to muster the depth of passion she'd had for Ethan. And what had that been, anyway? She barely knew him. He had a handsome face and a fit body. He was nice to her kids. That wasn't enough to explain the hideous wrench to her heart that she felt in his presence. She saw him as an escape, a distraction, and she'd called it love. Not a pleasant thought. All her life she'd hated people she perceived as shallow, yet what was she?

"Fuck this," she said to the large empty room, to the moonlight, and to the world beyond.

Patty did her share of soul searching, too, though never at night, because she was a hard sleeper. She saw marriage differently now. Married couples had a look to them, a quality other couples, even long-standing ones, simply didn't possess. She couldn't quite define it, but she always recognized it. The way they talked without looking at each other over dinner, how they finished one another's sentences. A look of security, as if the future were long and clear. And when people knew you were married, it was as if you joined a club, or crossed the border into a country where everyone spoke the same language. Then there was the power of the ceremony itself, where you stood up and said, *This person is important to me and I'm in it for the long haul.* A public declaration, like a judge being sworn into office. Being willing to uphold a sacred trust.

All of which led her one morning to say, "Marry me."

Murph sat behind the newspaper. After a moment, the paper lowered. His expression was bland. He thought he understood why she wanted him to now, after all this time.

"Feeling your age," Murph said.

"Well, I'd hardly be the blushing bride."

"Or the one eight months pregnant."

"How true."

"Aren't you going to get down on one knee?" Murph asked.

"Not after the week I had."

Something about a broken pipe at the restaurant.

"Okay, then. How about my ring?" Murph asked.

"You got one." A little silver band they found ages ago in Vegas. Hers had the same crisscross pattern. They'd wanted rings then, and not the rest of it.

She went to call Potter. Yes, she was sure she wanted the ceremony in Dunston. She'd need help, though. Potter didn't know where to start. Angie was busy at work. Timothy was sullen. The twins wouldn't be interested, and Foster, well, you didn't ask a seventeen-year-old boy to plan a wedding. That left Lavinia. Potter said he'd ask her himself. Patty said to ease into it, and give her a chance to get used to the idea.

"Give her a call in a day or two. I'll have talked to her by then," Potter said.

"Thanks, Big Brother."

"Anytime."

Angie was delighted when Patty asked her to be her maid-of-honor. Her boss, Bonita, told her to be sure and catch the bouquet. Angie had given up on finding love. After Professor Rawls and Brett, she was tired. She was twenty-five. Women in the novels she sometimes read from the nineteenth century found themselves on similar ground. Celibacy wasn't the end of the world, but Bonita wouldn't leave it alone. *You're missing out,* she'd say. *Join a club. Follow your interests. You'll see, there are lots of good fish in the sea.* As far as Angie knew, Bonita, also single, went straight home every day after work and sat down in front of the television set. She brought Angie with her one night for dinner. They ate on trays watching the news. Angie felt like an old woman, until Bonita started drinking. Then she felt like a younger caretaker. It was awkward giving gentle rebukes to her hostess, but Bonita really put it away. Angie was certain she'd be too hungover in the morning to function at work. She was wrong. Bonita showed no sign of the previous night's drinking. That meant she made it a habit, no doubt a daily one. She apparently had no trouble drinking the way she did and advising her clients to quit whatever substance they enjoyed—legal or illegal. Angie didn't think her a hypocrite. Rather, she understood that Bonita drank to decompress, the way Angie used the comfort of her quiet home for the same reason.

Her mother also gave her advice. Once it was all about her flaws—the weight she needed to lose, the ugliness of the piercings and tattoos she had indulged in as a teenager, her chronic bad temper. Now it was about love and companionship. *Find someone who makes you laugh. Don't worry if he doesn't make a lot of money. You want a guy you can spend all your time with and not get bored.* Angie knew that her mother was really talking about herself. She didn't light up around Chip the way she used to. If Chip noticed, he didn't say so. Angie shared her thoughts with her father.

"I wonder if they'll get divorced," she said. They were eating dinner. Potter no longer lived with her, but in his own little place over in Lansing. A tiny rental home overlooking a fallow field. In winter it lay under white. In spring it came into green, and by summer's end it gave up rolled balls of threshed hay. He used it to mark time. When another chunk of it had passed, he dropped by and cooked dinner. Tonight it was chili, his stand-by. Angie hated chili. She added extra sour cream to hers to soften the heavy spices Potter used.

"She'd be a fool to," he said.

"She's unhappy."

"Why? She got what she wanted."

Potter wasn't bitter. He was just being practical. She wanted money, she got it. She wanted security, she got that, too. She wanted a man who'd be there when she needed him, and Chip was surely that. To his way of thinking, a person's wants didn't change over time, since he wanted what he always had—the love of a good woman, a nice home, and a happy family. And to be able to respect himself, which had come in time.

"She doesn't love him," Angie said.

"Maybe love's not what she's good at."

When Angie was very young, her mother wrapped her arms around her, wiped her face, and put her to bed. Sometimes her words were gentle. Often she was silent. A firm-faced woman moving through the place with busy, efficient hands. Sewing buttons on shirts. Washing chipped dishes clean. Sweeping to a private, easy rhythm every corner of their little house. A time of laughing in whatever living room was temporarily theirs. Her dark hair swaying. Angie loved that hair, and how her mother brushed it to make it shine. Sometimes she let Angie touch it. To leave her hair down like that was an intimacy the rest of her denied. Then her hair was always up, the gentle words turned hard, and there was no more laughter. Was that when her love for her father disappeared, too? And she decided that love wasn't worth pursuing?

"She's bored. That's her problem," Angie said. She pushed her bowl of chili away and dabbed her lips with her napkin. Potter nodded. He sipped his iced tea. He didn't allow himself to drink alcohol with dinner, and not at all on most days.

"Bet you're right about that."

Angie knew she'd gotten to the truth of the matter. Her mother had worked so hard and for so long that to be at leisure now made her miserable.

"She needs a hobby," Angie said.

"You mother's not the hobby kind."

Angie had to agree. What, then? What would shake her out of her rut and make her enjoy life again?

"She thinks I should volunteer," Lavinia said. She and Chip were riding in his golf cart around the back lawn. They had just over two acres on that side of the house, while the front yard was actually fairly narrow. Chip liked to keep tabs on the gardener, whom he suspected of drinking on the job. Liquor bottles that didn't belong to him showed up in the recycle bin, according to Alma. Chip's bad ankle made the cart necessary, though Lavinia thought if he made a little more effort to use it, it would strengthen in time. They'd seen Angie for dinner the evening before. Angie mentioned a new program working with at-risk children after school. They always need people, she said.

Lavinia thought that was rich. After raising five of her own, she was supposed to spend time with someone else's? Yet she knew that's not what Angie meant at all.

"Yes, she mentioned that. I think you'd be good at it," Chip said. He brought the cart to a halt in front of a boxwood hedge. He surveyed the top. It wasn't level, but rose and fell in small dips and mounds.

"I'm not patient enough," Lavinia said. She got out of the cart, too. The sun was warm and the air was cool. Patty was due the following day.

"You're anything you want to be. It's up to you." Chip didn't say this meanly.

"I don't have anything to contribute. Not really."

"You sound as if you feel sorry for yourself."

"I do not!"

Chip took out a small tape measure from his pants pocket and lined it up next to an azalea bush. He'd requested that they be kept no taller than two feet. Three of the four that clustered by the west end of the boxwood hedge were well over that.

"That does it," he said.

"Relax."

"The hell I will."

"Don't fire him."

"Can't be helped."

"Because your bushes are too tall?"

"Because he doesn't follow orders."

"He's an old man, Chip. You can't just fire him."

"You don't know anything about business, Lavinia."

She reminded him how well she'd done working for him back in the day, and how often he'd told her just the opposite, that she had a good head for figures and was an asset to his company.

"Maybe I was just flattering you," he said.

"Were you?" Lavinia was flushed. Her eyes were dark and snapping.

"Yes."

She swung at him and he stepped aside. She was surprised he was so nimble and quick on his feet. He laughed at her. He was actually having fun! He held up his fists like a boxer in a ring and danced around. Then his bad ankle turned, and he went down on one knee with a groan.

"Damn it!" he said. Lavinia watched without offering any help. She wanted to kick him, she was so mad. Then she hauled him up. His slacks were muddy. He looked down at her, the amusement no longer in his eyes.

"I hope you know I was just kidding," he said.

"About the gardener?"

"About you not knowing anything about business."

"Didn't sound like it to me."

"You should know me better than that."

She stood with crossed arms.

"You've lost your sense of humor, Lavinia. Maybe that's why you're so out of sorts these days."

He turned away from her and got into the golf cart. He started the engine and drove off slowly without giving her a chance to get in, too. She supposed that was fair, under the circumstances. She *had* lost her sense of humor, and maybe that's the one and only thing Chip really liked about her.

Murph needed a drink. He hated to fly. He wanted to drive out to Dunston, and Patty wouldn't hear of it. So they took one plane from Helena to Chicago, then another to Buffalo, and a third tiny one from there to Dunston. Patty loved every minute of it. Murph practiced deep breathing and visualizing warm sandy beaches. It didn't work. By the time they arrived at Chip and Lavinia's, his hands were shaking and his mouth was so dry that it was hard to swallow. Murph tended to suffer more after something had happened than when it was actually going on. He headed straight for the liquor in Chip's study. Chip didn't mind. He enjoyed Murph's company.

Lavinia was in the kitchen carving up a cold leg of lamb. She wanted to keep her hands busy. She was anxious about the wedding and had asked Angie to call the rental company that was providing the chairs for the long table, and to check once more with both the florist and the caterer. Chip's friend Judge Logan, who'd conduct the ceremony, had already confirmed that he'd be there at three.

"Well, the way you're hacking up that poor thing makes me wonder if I should hightail it right back the way I came," said Patty. She smiled broadly. Lavinia stopping carving.

"How was your trip?" she asked.

"That fool of mine white-knuckled it the whole way."

"Hm."

"He's taking the edge off in there with your better half."

"At this time of day?"

"You know Murph."

Patty's eyes were as blue as her turquoise necklace. Her white top had puffed sleeves, something a much younger woman would wear, Lavinia thought. Then she realized that Patty felt young, probably because she was about to get married. Or because her life had worked out and she was happy. *Guess what?* Lavinia wanted to say. *I'm still in love with your brother.* That was last night's revelation. It hadn't surprised her one bit. She'd known it all along, really. And if she told Patty the truth right now, it wouldn't surprise her, either.

"You look good," Patty said.

"Thanks."

Patty put her huge purse on the floor. Something clanked from inside it.

"Napkin rings," Patty said.

"Oh?"

"Forgot to wrap them."

"You didn't need to bring me a hostess gift."

"Didn't say they were for you."

Lavinia stared at her.

"Kidding," Patty said.

Lavinia continued with her carving. She didn't invite Patty to sit down. Patty sat, anyway.

"We're all ready. The flowers should be here first thing tomorrow. And Angie's chasing down the caterer," Lavinia said.

"That sounds great. We're grateful for all you've done."

"Save your gratitude for later. The caterer's a nitwit. If everything comes off as planned, you can thank me then."

Patty watched Lavinia work the lamb. Bits of it were scattered over

183

the marble countertop. Patty wasn't much of a red meat eater, herself. Lavinia wasn't either, she remembered. So she was doing this on someone else's behalf. That was like her, Patty thought. Putting herself out, and not being so nice about it.

"Feels strange to think I'm getting married tomorrow," Patty said.

"Nervous?"

"Not really." Patty was, though, and refusing to let anyone know. Murph would tease her. Nicely, of course.

"The last wedding I went to was yours and Potter's," she said. Lavinia put her knife down.

"Wasn't much of an affair," she said.

"Sure it was. You and Potter, at your folks' place in the country. That flower in your hair, what was it?"

Lavinia went to the sink to wash her hands. Her eyes were wet and it was a bit hard to see.

"Lilac, I think," she said. She went on washing her hands, slowly and very thoroughly.

"Hydrangea, wasn't it?"

"That's right."

Chip and Murph appeared. They looked jolly. Lavinia was surprised to see Chip smile. He seldom smiled. He caught her eye. He stopped smiling.

"What's wrong?" he asked her.

"Nothing. Why?"

"You look upset."

"Don't be silly. I'm fine."

Chip went on watching Lavinia. Murph helped himself to some of the cut-up lamb.

"You're a pig," Patty told him.

"Oink," he said.

Murph went on eating until Patty told him to stop. She ordered him to take a shower, and not to have anything more to drink until evening.

"Ball and chain," he told Chip on his way out. Patty went with him. She wanted to unpack.

Lavinia cleaned up the counter. Chip stood where he was, not helping. Lavinia put the sponge in the sink.

"God damn it! I broke a nail," she said.

"I wish you'd let Alma do her job."

"I'm perfectly capable of wiping my own counters."

"I never said otherwise."

Chip smoothed down his thinning hair. Lavinia took him in then, all at once, a good hard look she hadn't given him for a long time. Her heart filled with affection. He'd been good to her.

"What?" he said.

"Nothing."

"I know I've put on a little weight. Thanks for not saying so."

"I didn't notice."

"Oh." He sounded disappointed.

Lavinia walked out past him and gave him a gentle pat on the arm. She remembered that Potter was on his way over to see Patty, and she didn't want to be there when he arrived.

She was cold. The top of the convertible was down, and she could put it up but didn't want to. There was something to be said for being uncomfortable, because when you were warm again you could remember being cold and wishing you weren't. When she felt bored or stuck, which was more or less all the time, she went shopping and didn't buy what she wanted because she pretended she couldn't afford to. It was a way of forcing herself into a state of being grateful, and if not grateful, then at least not dissatisfied. She made the mistake of sharing this concept once with Angie. She didn't recall the exact circumstances, something about wearing a pair of worn out shoes in the rain, maybe. The water leaking through a break in the sole. How wonderful it was to replace them and have dry feet. *There's more to life than spending money, Mom,* Angie had said.

Beside her in the passenger seat, her cell phone rang. Probably Chip wanting to know where she was. She didn't answer. When the phone stopped ringing, she turned it off. Chip could carry on without her. He had nothing to do that day, as usual. Patty and Potter would hang out and reminisce. Murph would occupy the study and drink slowly all afternoon although Patty had told him not too, and Chip would join him. They'd talk about Murph's getting married, and how wonderful that was. Chip would say that marrying Lavinia was the best thing he'd ever done, and Murph might just believe him. Then Chip would bring up the matter of Timothy, who was doing less with himself all the time, and didn't even show up regularly for the job Chip got him at his car dealership. Lavinia suspected drugs were involved, but she couldn't be sure. Angie had hinted at the same thing. *Sometimes he's just fine, then he's all giddy and spaced out.* Chip wondered if maybe some time out west with Murph as mentor would help. Lavinia wasn't keen for that. They shipped Angie off once, and she came home in a worse way than when she left, but perhaps it would be different with Timothy. Timothy simply needed a firm hand from someone he feared. Murph could be intimidating, not because he was cruel or mean, but because he was blunt and didn't mince words. Summer was a good time for such a venture, Chip figured. He imagined lots of time spent outdoors, doing physical labor. Murph had built a decent business for himself renovating homes. Chip hoped Timothy could learn something and turn into a man by virtue of working with his hands. Lavinia thought Chip was foolish. He'd never worked with his own hands, whereas she had. All those years taking care of Potter and her children had taught her that there was no virtue in being someone else's slave. In fact, it was a condition one tried like hell to escape.

She came to a five-way intersection. While she waited for her turn to go, she thought about where to drive next. The clouds were lowering and with any luck, rain would break loose. Then she could put the roof up and stop this odd chill that had crept inside of her. She took a sharp left, onto the street where she and Potter once lived in a house so small it was more like a cottage. One bedroom, one bathroom, and a tiny sitting area in front of the fireplace. They were happy there. Lavinia was pregnant with Angie. Potter had a job with the school system as a custodian. He didn't drink too much. They never argued. He'd stand behind her while she washed the dishes and put his hands on her growing stomach. She adored his touch. She adored him.

There was no place to park in front of the house, so she went down the block until she found room. She put the car's roof up. Rain had just then begun to fall. She walked along the sidewalk, shocked at the power of her memories.

The house was painted yellow. In their day it had been blue. The shutters were missing from one of the two front windows. The other window was cracked at the bottom. Beer bottles and concrete blocks littered the plot of grass that had been their lawn and garden. Daffodils and tulips bloomed so faithfully that first year. After Angie was born, Lavinia didn't plant any more bulbs. She was too tired. And resentful, too. Potter got fired and they had to ask her father for money. Potter said the school district was downsizing. Lavinia didn't believe him. Sometimes he went out with friends and didn't come home until late. He made up excuses. Somebody was too drunk to drive, he said, so he got him home safely. Later Lavinia learned that the person Potter was supposed to have escorted home hadn't even been at the poker game. She never thought it was another woman. He usually just lost track of time and made things up so she wouldn't get mad. She punished him for it and pushed him further and further away.

Yet love remained. Maybe if there had been fewer children, more money, or both, it would have been enough.

"Pipe dreams," she said. She forced herself not to cry. Inside the house, a telephone rang and rang. What a lonely sound, she thought. Unless someone was calling with bad news. In that case, the emptiness of the place was a mercy.

She went back towards the car. The rain stopped. A tall oak tree that had been there before pushed up the slate sidewalk with its roots. She fell and tore the knees of her linen pants. Her sunglasses flew off her face.

"Son of a bitch!" Her left knee bled. She pushed herself up. Her sunglasses were nowhere. A man carrying a briefcase crossed the street and approached her at a quick pace.

"You okay over there?" he called. Lavinia didn't answer. He asked her again when he reached her.

"Where did you come from?" she asked. He was tall, with horn-rimmed glasses. A professor maybe, though not likely in this neighborhood. Probably a city worker. The municipal offices were at the end of the block. Her question seemed to confuse him.

"It's just that I didn't see anyone around," she said.

"You should clean that up," he said, meaning her knee.

"Yes."

She took a better look at him. He was familiar. The glasses and the tie. "I sold you a manufactured home a few years ago, didn't I?"

"I believe you did," he said.

"Mr. Carson."

"Carlin. You were close."

"You don't look like the kind of guy who'd live in a trailer, if you don't mind my saying so."

"I bought it for my son. He'd just gotten out of jail."

It was odd to hear such frank news from a relative stranger.

"That was very generous of you," she said. Her knee hurt like hell. She glanced around for her missing sunglasses.

"Yes, well. Didn't do much good. He's back inside now," he said.

"I'm sorry."

"Probably just as well."

Lavinia understood what he meant. When you can't help someone who's a mess, it's better to let him pay for his mistakes. She thought of Timothy. He'd gotten detained by a store security guard last year for shoplifting an expensive leather jacket. No charges were filed because Chip intervened. Lavinia almost wished he hadn't.

"I didn't mean to keep you. You should really get that taken care of," he said.

"Yes, I will, thanks."

He looked into the distance, then walked back across the street. When he was out of sight, Lavinia went on her way, too.

She opened the door to the sound of laughter. There were people in the living room. She went into the kitchen and dabbed her torn knee with a paper towel and warm water. The sting made her bite the inside of her cheek.

"Is that you?" Chip called out. Lavinia continued her dabbing. A minute later Chip came into the kitchen. He had a glass of champagne in his hand. She assumed that he meant to give it to her. He didn't. He stopped smiling when he saw the shape she was in.

"What the hell happened to you?" he asked.

"Nothing."

"Looks like something."

"Just a little fall. It's not important. Who's here?"

"What? Oh, everyone. Potter, Angie, Murph and Patty."

"Wasn't Timothy supposed to come and say hello?"

"He was."

"Where are the girls?"

"Out, I think."

"Foster?"

"He came down to check in, then retreated back to his lair."

Too many people to keep track of. That's my problem, she thought.

"We tried calling you," Chip said.

"My battery ran down. What did you want?"

"To say we were starting the party early."

Lavinia threw the paper towel away. She opened her purse, which she'd left on the kitchen table, and took out a comb. She pulled it through her hair. The fall had sent it all around her face. Maybe Mr. Carlin thought she was drunk.

I always assume the worst.

Someone had opened the shutters in the living room, and the light fell in brilliants bars across the huge oriental rug. The sky must have cleared just in the few minutes Lavinia had been home. Everyone turned to look at her.

"Wow. Would it be fair to say that the other guy looks worse?" Patty asked.

"I tripped."

"Do you want to take a moment and go change?" Chip asked.

"No. But I will have a glass of that champagne."

Angie brought her one. "Are you sure you're okay?" she asked.

"I wish everyone would stop asking me that."

"So sit down and enjoy your drink," Potter said. He had on a crisp white shirt with rolled-up sleeves, and dark slacks with a firm crease down the legs. He smiled at her. Lavinia sat down. Murph and Patty were giggling on the couch, side by side. They seemed to be remembering something funny that happened a long time ago, involving a broken down truck and an old man who helped them out. They borrowed his phone, and his house was decorated with the small sculptures he made in his spare time, each one a hippopotamus that he painted in bright colors. A yellow one sat on the kitchen counter next to the phone, and Murph had trouble keeping a straight face when he called for a tow truck. They had just gotten together, and that day kicked off a lifetime of hilarity and chaos.

"Do you remember when the plumbing froze in the old house and we wrapped the baby's blanket around the kitchen faucet, trying to thaw it out?" Lavinia asked Potter.

"What?"

She repeated the question. He looked vague as he tried to recall what she meant.

"What old house?" he asked.

"The first one we lived in, on State Street."

She saw that he did remember then, but found her question peculiar. He turned his head back to Patty and Murph, who were still talking and laughing about the old man. Angie looked at Lavinia for a moment. The way her eyebrows came together said she was concerned.

"Potter," Lavinia said, not loudly enough for him to hear over the others.

"Potter!" she said, loudly.

"What?"

She froze. Everyone looked at her. Patty was in mid-smile. Her eyes were wet with laughing.

"Do you want another glass of champagne?" Lavinia asked.

"Haven't finished this one yet, but thanks."

Chip left the side chair he'd occupied to join Lavinia on the loveseat that faced the couch. He patted her undamaged knee.

"We don't have to stick around. We could go somewhere, if you like," he whispered.

"Like where?"

"Upstairs."

She stared at him. He meant it. The glow in his eyes was proof. Her heart sank.

"That wouldn't be very nice, would it?" she whispered back.

"Look at the lovebirds, with their heads together," Murph said.

Lavinia blushed. Angie poured him another glass, and one for Patty, too. She held up the bottle to ask if Lavinia and Chip wanted more. Lavinia didn't. Chip did.

"Two happy couples," Murph said. "Isn't that nice? Don't you think that's nice?" he asked Patty.

"Chill," she said. She looked at Potter. "We need to fix you up, Potter. You and Angie both. This single life you two lead is no good."

"Dad's got a girlfriend," Angie said. The conversation stopped for a moment. Potter looked pleased with himself.

"Who?" Patty asked.

"Someone he works with," Angie said.

"Estelle's her name," Potter said. From the way he said it, he was smitten. Lavinia wanted to crush the glass in her hand.

"When did all this happen?" Patty asked.

"Been going on for a while."

"Congratulations. Will there be another wedding any time soon?"

"You never know!"

The talk went on, and so did the drinking. The telephone rang and no one answered it. Lavinia kept her eye on Potter until he turned her way once more. She tried to recall his exact expression later, and each time hoped it conveyed his constant love for her. In her honest moments, which still came in the early hours, she knew it had shown only surprise.

ABOUT THE AUTHOR

photo © John Christiansen

A nne Leigh Parrish's debut story collection, *All The Roads That Lead From Home*, (Press 53, 2011) won the 2012 Independent Publisher Book Awards silver medal for best short story fiction. Her work can be found or is forthcoming in *The Virginia Quarterly Review, Clackamas Literary Review, The Pinch, American Short Fiction, Storyglossia, PANK, Prime Number, Bluestem, Crab Orchard Review, Literary Orphans, Spartan,* and *r.kv.r.y.*, among other publications. She is the fiction editor for *Eclectica Magazine*. She lives in Seattle. To learn more, visit her at www.anneleighparrish.com.